In Sheep's
Clothing

ALSO BY RETT MACPHERSON

Blood Relations

Killing Cousins

A Misty Mourning

A Comedy of Heirs

A Veiled Antiquity

Family Skeletons

In Sheep's Clothing

A NOVEL BY

RETT MACPHERSON

ST. MARTIN'S MINOTAUR

NEW YORK

1837 2027

www.minotaurbooks.com

Library of Congress Cataloging-in-Publication Data

MacPherson, Rett.
    In sheep's clothing / Rett MacPherson.—1st St. Martin's Minotaur ed., 1st U.S. ed.
        p. cm.
    ISBN 0-312-30178-2
    1. O'Shea, Torie (Fictitious character)—Fiction.   2. Women genealogists—Fiction.   3. Swedish Americans—Fiction.   4. Women immigrants—Fiction.   5. Minnesota—Fiction.   6. Diaries—Fiction. I. Title.

PS3563.A325715   2004
813'.54—dc22

2003061178

First Edition: February 2004

10 9 8 7 6 5 4 3 2 1

To the members of the Alternate
Historians: Tom Drennan,
Laurell K. Hamilton, Debbie Millitello,
Sharon Shinn, and Marella Sands.
My buddies, my pals, and the
best darn critique group west
of the Mississippi.

Acknowledgments

The author wishes to acknowledge those who have helped her bring this book to publication.

First of all I would like to thank the folks—mostly family—in Minnesota: Jean and Gary Erickson, Mike and Lavonne Sparks, Aaron and Rachel Remig, Hans and Sherry Sparks, Bobby Sparks, and Tara and Shawn Raftery. All of the Pecarinas: Dan, Mary Kaye, Alan, and Jenny; and the Edmans: Mary Lou, Nikki, and Betsy. Without you guys I wouldn't know anything about Minnesota, nor would I have anybody to visit! Thanks for sparking my interest and answering the endless questions; unfortunately a lot of what I've learned didn't even make it into this book.

Thank you to everybody at Writers House, Michele Rubin, and Merrilee Heifetz, and all of the people at St. Martin's Press who do a wonderful job on my books. In particular, my editor, Kelley Ragland and her assistant, Benjamin Sevier.

Thank you to my husband, Joe, for putting up with me and in general helping out when I'm "cramming" pages.

Big thank you to Sharon Shinn who keeps asking for more, and, in general, couldn't be more supportive.

And thanks to you readers who keep the series going.

In Sheep's
Clothing

One

"Really, Torie. Have you gained weight?"

I just stared at my stepfather, Sheriff Colin Brooke, hoping that his head would burst into flames. I was sandwiched in between him and my husband, Rudy, in the front seat of Rudy's truck, on our way to Minnesota for a fishing excursion and a visit to my most favorite aunt in the world. Colin twisted and turned on the passenger side of the truck, trying to scratch an itch on his back. Colin has always been a strapping man, and it seemed that he was getting bigger with every year. The audacity of him to suggest that I was the one who had gained weight!

"Let me tell you something, Colin. *You* now live with the greatest cook in the world—who happens to be my mother—not me. When was the last time *you* stepped on a scale?"

"Now, now, Torie," Rudy said. Rudy was always the peace-keeper and the first to tell me when I was jumping to conclusions. Even though I know this about him, it didn't make it easier to listen to him now.

"Oh, don't you even start," I said. "He just called me fat and you're going to take his side?"

"He did not call you fat, and I'm not taking his side," Rudy said.

I folded my arms, made some disgruntled sound, and watched as silo number fifty-four went by. Iowa is not boring, contrary to popular belief. In fact, it's quite pretty. All of the rolling farmland stretching out into the distance is very soothing to the eye. At least for me, anyway. But I've always loved farmland and I've always loved the subtle rolling charm of the Midwest.

My aunt Sissy had called a few weeks ago to ask if I would come up for a visit. She had sounded a bit odd, but then Aunt Sissy always sounds odd. But this time there had been just a bit more urgency in her voice and a touch of . . . worry. At any rate, Rudy hadn't been able to pass up the chance to spend a week in the land of ten thousand lakes. Actually, there are almost twelve thousand lakes, but I guess rounding it down to ten thousand was catchier for bumper stickers and license plates. Believe me, there is no other person on the planet, other than my dear aunt Sissy, for whom I would deliberately squeeze myself between the two biggest fishermen west of the Mississippi, nor was there another person for whom I would put myself in the line of fire of Sheriff Colin Woodrow Brooke for thirteen straight hours with no reprieve.

Fifteen minutes later Colin tried to scratch his itch again. "We should have gone through Wisconsin," he said.

Most people who go to Minnesota from eastern Missouri would go through Illinois to Wisconsin to Minnesota, but it added extra miles and an extra hour to the trip. It's just that, well, there's an actual highway to take if you go through Wisconsin. I feel comfortable on two-lane roads, but most people prefer highways. And besides, every time I take the Wisconsin route I always get off on the wrong exit and end up in Chicago first.

"The Wisconsin route takes you way out of your way," Rudy said.

"Yeah, but there's no place to stop and eat in this state," Colin said, flailing his arms all about. "How can there be so much . . . so much *nothing?* There's miles and miles of nothing."

"There are plenty of places to eat," I said. "If you only eat three meals in one day."

"And what is that supposed to mean?" Colin asked.

"It means that you eat ten meals a day. I swear, if you were shorter, I'd think you were a hobbit," I said.

"Okay, that's it," Colin said. "Let me out."

"Colin," Rudy chastised.

"She just called me a hobbit!" he yelped. "I don't have to put up with this. Let me out."

"You're going to walk to Minnesota?" I asked, laughing. To think, I could have called him something a lot worse than a hobbit.

"It beats the heck out of traveling with you!" he snapped.

Being trapped in the cab of a truck with Colin would be enough to do a lot of people in, except my mother, who loved him, and my husband, who could talk fishing lures and bait and tackle forever with this man. The fact that I couldn't get away from him seemed to make my fuse shorter and my tolerance nil.

"Well, nobody invited you," I said. "You heard Rudy say he

3

was going fishing in Minnesota and you just assumed that meant you were going."

"You know, I always thought Rudy was a saint, but now I *know* he's a saint!"

"Oh, that is just so typical of a man," I said and huffed. "Rudy, pull over and feed him so he'll stop barking."

In response to that, Colin could do nothing but sputter and spew and look out the window with so much venom it was as if he were trying to melt the glass. I know he's the sheriff and all, but it was really difficult to take him seriously when he was wearing a pin on his fishing cap that read: FISHERMEN DO IT IN THE RIVER.

"Okay, stop it," Rudy said to me. His beautiful brown eyes held no humor this time. He was genuinely annoyed. "You're behaving like our children. You'd ground the girls for fighting like this."

"Yes, but he—"

"What? He started it? Oh, come on, Torie. Come up with something more original than that."

Colin cast his eyes to see me without turning his head. He was smug and happy that I had been properly chastised. And I didn't care what Rudy said, I still wanted Colin's head to burst into flames. I mean, you just don't ask a woman if she's gained weight and expect to live.

"I don't believe this," I said.

"And as for you, Colin," he said, "you're not on duty, so quit acting like you can just boss everybody around. And next time you're hungry, just say you're hungry so we can stop, rather than huffing and puffing and pouting and shifting and complaining about taking the Iowa route. Okay?"

"Whatever," Colin said. Without missing a beat his eyes

4

caught a glimpse of a sign and he nearly lurched out of his seat belt. "Oh, there's a Pizza Ranch at this exit!"

•

So, obviously, we stopped at the Pizza Ranch, which is like a Ponderosa buffet, only with pizza. Colin must have eaten two whole pizzas, but there was no way to tell since he could claim that two of the seven times he got up, he had actually gone to the rest room. No sense in arguing with the man. I knew how much pizza he had eaten. We were back on the road after what seemed like a two-hour meal, only to stop two more times for gas, once to get more food at a drive-thru, and five times so that I could get my french vanilla cappuccino refilled. I never drink coffee; in fact, I like my caffeine cold. But on a trip like this, the only thing that kept my eyelids from plastering shut was the real stuff.

The thirteen-hour trip to my aunt Sissy's house along the St. Croix river turned into a seventeen-hour trip due to the fact that we had to stop and feed the horse known as Colin Brooke. As a result we didn't get into my aunt's house until about four in the morning, when I had expected to be there by midnight. I could only hope that she wasn't up waiting for us, because I would feel incredibly guilty and then I'd have another reason to be mad at Colin.

When the lights from our truck flashed across a sign that read MORGAN FARMS AND NURSERY my heart gave a little skip. I was like a giddy schoolgirl, so excited to get to see one of my most favorite relatives. I was a little concerned, though. Aunt Sissy had called and left a message on our machine that said, "This is your aunt Sissy. I need some help. Come up for a week." She hadn't even given me time to answer. The next

5

morning she called and said, "You comin' or not? I'm an old lady and I don't have as much time as you." That was Sissy Morgan for you. Gruff and brusque, to the point, and brutally honest. But I adore her nonetheless. Maybe it is just because she is so different from most of the people in my family.

But, still, I couldn't help but wonder why she needed my help. If it was feeding the horses or pulling weeds, not a problem. I'd be out there at the crack of dawn. Our conversation had held a clear underlying urgency, but not to the degree that I could question her about it. And that worried me.

Rudy pulled the truck onto a gravel road that had deep ravines cut in it. Off to the left was a two-story Victorian home, surrounded by outbuildings, fencing, animals, greenhouses, and fields on top of fields of growing things. The front porch light was lit and a small lamp glowed in the front living room.

"That's it!" I exclaimed. "That's her house."

Five minutes later we were standing on the front porch with our suitcases, smelling the country air and feeling the nip of spring on our cheeks. May in Minnesota is a bit cooler and wetter than May in Missouri. There was a note on the door that read: "Obviously, you're late. If you're not up by six, you miss breakfast. Aunt S."

"Gee, what a warm welcome," Colin said.

"Listen here," I said. "You say one thing bad about my aunt Sissy and I *will* torture you."

Colin looked taken aback and then started to laugh.

"No, you don't understand," Rudy said. "She's serious."

"Oh."

"Come on," I said. "I know which ones are the guest rooms."

We entered the house, and the smell of cinnamon and nut-meg overwhelmed my senses. Her house always smelled so good. Ever since I was a child, I had imagined the smell of her house was what heaven must smell like. As we made our way up the stairs, I heard Colin talking to Rudy.

"Is she always like this?" Colin asked. "I mean, I've never seen another side to her. But I know there has to be one."

"Torie definitely has her good side."

"You're not just saying that?"

"No, I'm serious."

"That's good, because I worry about you."

Rudy laughed.

"What's so funny?" Colin asked.

"It's you I'm worried about. I can handle myself."

Colin made some smirking sound and I ignored them as best as I could. Tomorrow would be a better day. I wouldn't be trapped in a car with Colin, listening to him complain and discuss fishing lures for hours on end. I wouldn't be all cramped and cranky and I'd get to visit with my aunt and things would look better. Colin wouldn't annoy me as much, because he'd be in a boat out on a lake, miles away, and I'd be with Aunt Sissy. He couldn't annoy me if he wasn't around, right? Don't answer that. Yes, tomorrow would be a better day.

Even if it was only two hours away.

Two

It seemed as if I'd just shut my eyes when the alarm went off. Aunt Sissy had set both alarm clocks in the guest rooms so that we woke up at precisely six in the morning. For a split second, I thought I was still at home in New Kassel, Missouri, in my blue gingham bedroom, and the Mississippi tugboats charging by outside my window. But soon my eyes focused on my surroundings: the antique dresser, the beveled mirror, the watercolor portrait of my grandmother Keith's grandparents from France.

And then there was that smell . . .

Bacon, brown-sugar sausage links, eggs, warm maple syrup, biscuits, and coffee. I definitely was not in New Kassel. I hadn't woken up to breakfast being cooked downstairs since my mother married Colin and moved out. I realize, of course, that my mother had to move out if she was to get married, but Colin definitely got the better end of the deal. It had been instant oatmeal, Pop-Tarts, and cold cereal ever since. Sigh.

No matter how gritty my eyes felt, or how sunken they looked, the smell of breakfast cooking was enough to make my body get up and move. I yanked the covers back and swatted Rudy on the butt. "Rise and shine!"

"Yeah, yeah, yeah," he said and pulled the covers back up and over his head.

"Smell that?" I said and jumped on top of him.

"My nose doesn't work this early."

"Mmmmm, bacon and sausage and eggs . . ."

"You don't even eat sausage," he grumbled.

"That doesn't mean that it doesn't smell good."

"Go away."

I tickled his ribs and still he made no move to get up.

"There's a big swordfish out there with your name on it. Just waiting for you to catch it and eat it or mount it or whatever it is you're going to do with it. Although, if you're going to mount it, you and I need to have a serious discussion about interior decorating."

"There are no swordfish in Minnesota," he said from under the covers.

"Whatever. There's a big fish out there just waiting for your worm. Okay, that didn't sound right. Just waiting for your bait and lures and stuff. Come on, get up," I said. I tugged on the blanket, but he had a death grip on it.

"Go away."

"Come on, you sound like Lon Chaney under there."

"And that's a bad thing?" he asked.

"Fine," I said. "But you know Colin is probably already down there eating all your food."

He sighed heavily and threw back the covers. "All right. Get off me."

I pulled on the jeans and sweatshirt from the drive up and then nearly skipped down the hallway and took the steps two at a time. I rounded the corner, ran into the kitchen, and threw my arms around my aunt Sissy. "I've missed you!"

She hugged me back, a batter-covered spatula in her hand nearly hitting me in the head. "Beginning to think you weren't coming," she said.

"Well, you know—"

"I know. You had to stop and feed that one," she said and pointed to Sheriff Brooke, already seated at her table and partaking of a breakfast fit for a king. He smiled and had the decency to blush.

"That's exactly right," I said. I was a little taken aback by Aunt Sissy's appearance. She was dressed as I've always seen her. Some Wal-Mart pullover shirt, jeans cut off at the calves, red high-top sneakers, and a baseball cap on her head. But she looked thinner. And a shadow had cast itself under her eyes and along her cheekbones.

She smiled and I instantly dismissed whatever it was that was niggling at my brain. "There's my favorite nephew-in-law," she said as Rudy shuffled into the kitchen and yawned. "You're only my favorite because you're married to Torie."

"I know," he said. "I love you, too." He hugged her and she returned the embrace with gusto.

"Can I help you with anything?" I asked.

"No. Just eat up. Your uncle Joe is out feeding the horses. You can go on out after you eat," she said. "He's expecting you."

"Sure," I said, feeling as if I were fifteen and had just been given license to do something reserved for big people.

"So, what kind of farm is this?" Colin asked.

"We sell chickens and eggs, and llamas."

"Huh?"

"Yeah, the llamas are good for keeping coyotes and predators away from other animals. So, farmers who have livestock, or sheep, turkeys, and chickens, all come to us for the llamas."

"Well," Colin said. "Never heard of such a thing."

Aunt Sissy just looked at him as if he were stupid. I, of course, didn't mention that I had never heard of llamas being sold to keep away predators either. I was enjoying the fact that she thought Colin was stupid. Why disrupt a perfect moment with the truth?

"Then we also have a market that we open when the crops come in. That's what the draught horses help with. Working the fields. Then, there's the nursery. People come and buy trees and shrubs and plants from us," she said. "We're getting too old to do it all by ourselves. So my two grandsons come up and work on the weekends and during the summers, and we pay them. But they can't touch the money until they graduate. I'm hoping they use it for college. But you know how stupid young people are."

"Sounds like a good living, anyway," Colin said. "Even if it is a lot of work."

"Oh sure," she said. "We've done this our whole lives, even before we moved up here, and we've never had to do the nine-to-five thing, and all the rush-hour traffic. That's just not for me, no way. You know, I've always said that people who live in big cities are only livestock. They simply don't realize it."

"That's a little harsh," Colin said.

"Whatever," she said. "I call it as I see it."

It disturbed me that Aunt Sissy had described herself and Uncle Joe as being too old to do all of the work by themselves.

What disturbed me was the fact that, indeed, they were pushing seventy. And that she was aware of it. It just seems so sad when a person realizes that the time of doing what they love is coming to an end. It wasn't as if they were going off to a nursing home anytime soon, but there were limitations to what they could do now. And even more limitations were to come.

Colin stretched and rubbed his belly. "This was an amazing meal."

"What did you think, only Jalena was capable of cooking a good meal?" Aunt Sissy asked.

"No, it's just . . . uh . . ."

"Bacon and sausage came from the neighbor's farm down the road. Eggs are ours. We made the syrup. All natural and fresh ingredients."

"Well, you can tell," he said.

"Darn right, you can tell."

Aunt Sissy turned her back and Colin rolled his eyes as if to indicate how seriously she took her breakfasts. I smiled, because that was the way she had always been. Nobody ever knew how to take her exactly.

"Coffee," Rudy said.

Aunt Sissy laughed and I shook my head. "He doesn't talk much until he's got enough caffeine in him to run the space shuttle," I said.

"Uncle Joe's not a morning person, either." She slammed a coffee mug in front of Rudy, filled it up with coffee, and gave a little laugh. Rudy picked up the mug without blinking and drank two gulps of hot coffee. He then closed his eyes, took a deep breath, and sighed.

"Good morning, lovely people!" he said.

"You're pathetic," I said.

"What?" he asked.

"Hey, I'm gonna run out and say hello to Uncle Joe," I said.

"You're not going to eat?" Aunt Sissy asked. "Don't tell me you're one of these weird women who don't eat breakfast?"

"No, I'm going to eat. I just want to go say hello. I'll be five minutes at the most."

"All right, but if your food gets cold, it's your fault."

I found my shoes by the door in the living room and stepped out onto the front porch. The floor of the porch was painted slate gray and its outer perimeter was surrounded by lilac bushes in full bloom. I thought about how weird it was that my lilac bush in the backyard had bloomed a month ago. In fact, as I looked out across the yard, I saw that the trees had that surreal green to them that they get right after the buds have just opened. I took a deep breath and smelled the greenness. As I stepped down onto the concrete step, I noticed something engraved in it. Nothing fancy—in fact, it looked as if somebody had just taken a tree branch and scribbled it: 1858. That's all it said.

I headed over to the stables and saw Uncle Joe as he was rounding the corner with a bucket full of water. "Hey, you need help with that?" I called out.

"Torie! Good to see you."

I ran up and gave him a hug, careful not to slosh the water all around. "Good to see you, too."

"How was the drive?" he asked.

"Could have been better, but I won't complain," I said. "Do you have another bucket?"

"Here, take this one, I'll go get the other one."

I took the bucket from him and headed into the stables. I was amazed at the sheer size of the draft horses in the barn.

Their heads alone were about as long as a three-year-old was tall. For the most part they ignored me, and I began looking for a place to empty the bucket. I stood there scratching my head, because I couldn't find a water trough to pour it in. Uncle Joe came back and realized my dilemma.

"Oh, down at the end, just outside the door."

I carried the bucket down the length of the stable and found the trough by the fence. I poured the water in and watched it mix with the water that was already in there. I always feel sorry for animals because their water is never clean. "How many horses do you have now?" I asked.

"Just the two Belgians. Eat me out of house and home."

"I bet," I said.

Uncle Joe recited how much food they ate in a day, how much water they drank, how much they cost to be shod, and so forth. It seemed as if he was just making small talk to avoid having to talk about the issue that was really bothering him. I could always sense when people were doing that.

I went along with it and asked a few questions about the horses. When I had run out of questions to ask, I asked the only thing I could think of. "So you've got llamas?"

"Yup, your aunt's idea."

"She's weird."

"Weirder than you know," he said. Uncle Joe was one of those all-around nice guys. Pleasant face, kind blue eyes, and a receding hairline that nearly reached the middle of his scalp. He seemed to always be busy and had a habit of talking when he had nothing to say. Sort of like me. I find that an endearing quality, but believe it or not, there are people who don't like it.

He glanced about nervously and finally decided to say what

it was that was on his mind. "Glad you're here, Torie. I'm worried about Sissy. You find out what's wrong with her. Okay?"

"If . . . if I can," I said, a little shocked.

He gave me the most pathetic look I've ever seen. It was almost as if he were crying without actually crying. "If you can't find out what's wrong, then nobody can."

Three

It was difficult going back into Aunt Sissy's house and eating breakfast as if Uncle Joe had not just said the oddest thing in the world to me. But I tried my best. Sometimes I think I deserve an Oscar for my performances. Subtlety is not my strong point, by any stretch of the imagination, but I can pretend that nothing is wrong if I have to.

Breakfast was great. I'm not sure how one woman could make scrambled eggs taste so much better than anybody else's, but she could. Rudy had gone upstairs to get ready to go fishing, but Colin was still sitting at the end of the long breakfast table. "What are you waiting for, scraps?" I asked.

"No," he said. "You know, you really should be nicer to me."

"Why?"

"Because it would make you a better person."

Before I could say anything, Aunt Sissy jumped in. "He's right, you know."

"I should be nicer to him?"

"I didn't say that," she said. "But it would make you a better person if you were. I, personally, would be mean as hell to him."

"Oh my God," Colin said to me, all wide-eyed. "There are two of you."

Aunt Sissy and I burst into laughter, and Colin couldn't hold it any longer and joined us. After he had regained control of himself, he rubbed his face with his hands and sighed. "I'm going fishing."

"Have fun," I said. "Don't drown."

"I'll try not to," he said as he left the kitchen.

"Don't get eaten by a crocodile or anything."

"Not a chance," I heard him say from the stairwell.

Aunt Sissy had finally sat down and begun eating her own breakfast. The farm wife always eats last, and it just doesn't seem fair, since she's the one who does all the work. Her kitchen was beautiful. Deep mahogany cabinets hung on two walls and blond wood made up the floor. It looked like pine of some sort. In Missouri, I worked for the historical society giving tours of the Gaheimer House, which is one of the oldest buildings in New Kassel. So I always notice things like beams in the ceilings, wood floors, and mouldings.

"I forgot how beautiful this house is," I said. I had visited her a handful of times since she moved up here twelve years ago.

"Yes," she said. "I love it. Sometimes I think it was built just for me, and the land surrounding it was created just for me."

"I've lived in New Kassel all my life," I said. "And I sort of feel the same way about it. Like, there's just no place else on earth that I would ever feel comfortable with. But I wonder sometimes if that's just because I've never known any other place."

"All I know," Aunt Sissy said, "is when we pulled into the driveway here, I really felt like I had come home."

"That's great," I said. Aunt Sissy had been born and raised in southeast Missouri, and lived thirty of her married years in that same area. The fact that she could move in her late fifties and find a place that she liked even better was comforting somehow. As if there's magic in the smallest corners of the universe.

"Of course, the house had been completely renovated," she said.

"Really?"

"The house that was originally built here is long gone. Well, not completely," she said. "The back porch and the cellar underneath it are still from the original homestead."

"How long ago was that?"

"Eighteen fifty-eight," she said.

"Oh," I said. "I saw those numbers carved in the front concrete."

She gave me a peculiar look and then smiled. "Yes, the steps are the original steps, too. The house burned down and all that survived was the back porch, the cellar, the front steps, and the chimney."

"Wow," I said. "When did it burn?"

"Not sure," she said. "But I know that the land and the ruins just sort of stood neglected for a while and then another house was built here in 1878, I think."

"Is that this house?"

"For the most part. They just built around the chimney and

the back porch and incorporated it into the new house. Isn't that odd?"

"Yeah, sort of. Maybe the person who built it just couldn't tear down what was left," I said.

"Well, anyway," she said, clearing her dishes. "There was a fire in that house, too, and it destroyed the far western part of the house. So they rebuilt it. If you walk down the hall toward the bedrooms, you can see where they added the new part after the fire. Because the floors are uneven."

"Oh, that's cool," I said. "I love things like that. It gives the house personality."

"Anyway, a family of thirteen lived here all during the Depression and the war years. Then it stood abandoned all through the sixties and seventies, and finally somebody bought it in the eighties and started renovating it. I mean, they just gutted the house and started from scratch."

"Wow," I said. "That's amazing."

Aunt Sissy put the dirty dishes into the dishwasher.

"You need some help with anything?" I asked.

"No," she said, putting detergent in the slot and slapping the door shut. She stood there a minute thinking about what to say next. "It took that family almost five years to renovate this house. They put it on the market and nobody bought it."

"Why? It's a gorgeous house."

"Well, at the time, it only came with a few acres. The place is hell and gone from any major city. I mean, we're practically smack-dab in between Duluth and the Twin Cities. It would be an impossible commute and there just aren't that many jobs around here that could support living in a house like this. I mean, they were asking a lot of money for the place," she said.

"So, how'd you get it?"

"After a few years, the family who owned the property next to it decided they wanted to sell off about a hundred acres. So, suddenly, if you put a hundred acres with this house, you've got a farm. Our real estate agent called us in the spring of 1990 and said that there was this place she knew of that had a hell of a house, with a hundred acres adjacent to it," she said. "The problem was it was in Minnesota."

"That's an amazing story," I said.

"Well, yes," she said. "Because we had told our real estate agent that we were willing to relocate out of state. We'd told her we would move to Colorado, Montana, Wyoming. We never said anything about Minnesota. She just happened across it and thought it was exactly what we were looking for. And it was. When we got here, there were repairs that needed to be done, because it had stood vacant for so long. Outbuildings had to be built. But we bought the hundred acres next to it and the house and have never regretted it one moment."

"Well, I think this house is you," I said. "My whole childhood, I remember you and Uncle Joe living on the farm in Ste. Genevieve. And I thought you guys were insane for moving up here. But then, when I came to see you the first time, I fell in love with it. And I remember thinking, well, of *course* she moved up here. Look at the place."

Aunt Sissy smiled.

"You must love it," I said. "Because you know a lot about its history. Most people can't tell you the name of the people who owned their houses before them, much less the history you just gave me. All the fires and everything. You must have done some research on it."

"Yeah," she said and looked out the window. She paused just a little too long, and it made me worry. "You seen the new quilt I'm working on?"

"No," I said.

"It's out there on the back porch."

"On the back porch? Won't the sunlight fade it?"

"Oh, I pull the shades when I'm not working on it. But there is nothing better than natural sunlight to quilt by," she said. "Go on. Go have a look."

"Okay," I said. I went out to the enclosed back porch to take a look at the quilt that she was working on. If I was not mistaken, it was a Lemoyne Star, done in earth tones. Greens, gold, browns. I rubbed my fingers across the stitches that she had most recently sewn. I couldn't be near a quilt and not touch it, just as I couldn't be near a piano and not run my fingers over the keys. Her stitches were so tiny. I had recently begun quilting. I have to admit, it's addictive, and I find myself buying fabric that I don't even have projects for. But I was nowhere near this good, and wasn't sure I ever would be.

Aunt Sissy came up behind me. "This is the porch that survived the first fire," she said and looked around.

"The quilt is gorgeous."

"Thank you," she said. "It's for you. I'm almost finished with it."

"Oh, Aunt Sissy," I said, chills dancing down my spine. "You can't give this to me."

"Sure, I can. I've quilted so many quilts in my life. All my kids got more quilts than they have beds to put them on. You can have this one. You've always been my favorite niece."

I swiped at a tear and hugged her. Her favorite niece. And that was saying something, considering my father's family was huge. There were many nieces and nephews to choose from. "Thank you," I managed to say.

"Don't go gettin' all misty on me," she said.

"Oh, of course not. Never," I said.

"You see that?" she asked and pointed to a small trapdoor in the floor.

"Yeah," I said.

"That was the cellar."

"Oh," I said, wondering why she was back to this subject. A peculiar feeling flowered in my chest.

"That was where she died," she said as if it were the obvious next step in the conversation.

"Where who died?"

She shrugged. "Not sure. Neighbor told me there was a girl who died during the first fire. She was in the cellar and died of smoke inhalation," she said.

"Oh, Aunt Sissy. Neighbors get things wrong," I said. "She might be overexaggerating."

She shrugged. "Maybe."

"Is there . . . are you . . . why are you telling me this? Is it bothering you that somebody may have died here? You can't let something like that ruin how much you love this place."

"Oh, no," she said. "That's not it."

"Well, what is it?"

"I don't know exactly," she said. She paused a moment and opened the back window, allowing a very cool, moist breeze to float across the quilt. "I just think it's a coincidence. And I hate coincidences."

"What's a coincidence?"

"Well, when the couple that renovated the place started working, they found some things—"

"Not bones, I hope. Please tell me they didn't find bones. Because that will ruin the place for me."

"No, they didn't find bones," Aunt Sissy said.

"Whew, good," I said with a sigh.

"There were things in the cellar and in one of the outbuildings, and they told me that they belonged to the family that lived here during the Depression," she said.

"Okay," I said, wondering just where she was going with this.

"Well, they put everything up in the attic and told me that I could do what I wanted with the stuff, since nobody really knew who it belonged to and nobody claimed it. That beveled mirror in the guest room that you're in was one of the items."

"Very pretty mirror," I said. I sounded like one of those birds. *Polly want a cracker. Very pretty mirror. Kaaawww.*

"So, I kept the stuff," she said.

"There's no law against that."

"One of the things I found was a book."

"A book. What kind of book?"

"Melodrama. You know, like one of those Brontë girls would write."

"Who was it by?"

"Don't know. That's part of the problem. It was written in longhand, still on paper. It was not bound or published. And there was no name on it."

She was driving me mad. Why didn't she just tell me what it was she wanted me to know? I stopped and thought a moment. Usually when people did this type of thing, it was because they were uncomfortable discussing whatever the subject was. "Did you read it?"

Color crept into her cheeks. Bingo. She had read it. She felt guilty about reading it.

"Yes," she said. "I read it."

"So, what's this got to do with the girl who died in the cellar?"

"I dunno," she said. "The book is about this young Swedish girl who moved to Minnesota and . . . she sort of has this torrid love affair. It's quite explicit in places," she said, and looked away. "And you can tell it's written in the old, old days. The handwriting, the things she talks about. I dunno. It just gave me a weird feeling."

"Why?"

"Because here's this novel about this young Swedish girl—written at least prior to 1890—and it was found in the cellar. And in that very same cellar a young girl had died. Just the coincidence of it disturbed me," she said.

"That's *if* a young girl really died in the cellar. If that part of the story is wrong, then there is no coincidence."

My aunt Sissy was pragmatic and practical. She was never prone to melodrama or overactive imagination, unlike her niece. For her to say that this "coincidence" gave her a weird feeling, it must truly have disturbed her.

"You'd have to read it," she said. Her eyes flicked nervously toward me. Alas, I had found what it was she was after.

"I'd love to read it. You want me to read it?"

Her whole body relaxed. "No," she said. "What I really want is for you to find out who wrote it."

"What?"

She was quiet a moment.

"Is that what you brought me up here for?" I asked. "Is this what you needed the help with?"

"I can't stand it, Torie. I can't stand not knowing who wrote that book. And I can't . . . It's not finished. The manuscript is incomplete. I'm hoping that if you can find out who wrote it, then maybe you can find out how it ends."

"Oh, Aunt Sissy, that's preposterous. The chances . . . Okay, even if I *could* figure out who wrote it, the chance that I'd ever be able to find out how the book ends is just a million to one. A needle in a haystack would have a better chance of being found than an ending to that book."

"You can do it, Torie. You do this sort of thing all the time."

Okay, she had me there. Aside from the tours that I give for the historical society, I am a genealogist, a historian, and a record keeper. I mean, this was my area of expertise. But, good Lord. To try and find the missing pages of a manuscript that had been written prior to 1900 . . . It made my head hurt just thinking about it.

"You do realize that if there was an end to the book, that it would be here somewhere on this property," I said to her. "And most likely destroyed by either of the fires or damaged by water."

"No," she said quickly. "I've thought about it. What if it actually got published? What if whoever wrote it moved and finished it somewhere else? Or just rewrote the whole thing. Or what if somebody took the end of the book when they moved, and just didn't realize they didn't take the whole thing. They could have it packed away somewhere."

She was certifiable. Years of never wearing socks and exposing her ankles had finally turned her brain to mush.

"Aunt Sissy . . ."

"You could try. The boys will be fishing. I will do whatever you want. I'll cook for you, take you places. You name it."

"Aunt Sissy . . ."

"You're the only person I know who can do this."

How could I say no? She was my most favorite aunt and she had never, not once in all the years I had known her, asked me for a favor. Not like this. Besides, it might be fun. "All right," I said. "I'll find out who wrote it. But I'm not promising anything else."

"Good enough," she said and smiled. "I have to know who wrote that book before I die."

With that she turned to walk outside into the brilliant sunshine that had begun to peek over the windbreak of conifers. It was entirely too early for this. If I were at home in Missouri, I'd just be getting the kids up for school. "Wait," I said, and stuck my head out the door. "First thing I need to do is read the manuscript."

"Of course," she said and came back in. "I get forgetful in my old age."

"Stop saying stuff like that," I said.

She just smiled and disappeared into the house. It appeared as though I would be spending most of the day reading.

Four

I read what I could at Aunt Sissy's kitchen table. Uncle Joe had told Rudy and Colin what lake to go to for the day's catch. Colin was pretty amazed that within forty miles there were three lakes to choose from. That's Minnesota for you.

"Is there anything I can get you?" Aunt Sissy asked me.

I thought a moment. "Well, if I'm going to be reading most of the day, you can go get me some Dr Pepper and a box of that Cheez-It Party Mix."

She gave me that look. The one that older people give you when they feel sorry for you because you don't eat right, or you don't get enough exercise. "Didn't your mother teach you that pop is nothing but sugar water?"

"And caffeine. You mustn't forget the caffeine."

She rolled her eyes. "Anything else?"

"No, that should do it for now. Oh, but I do need a pen and some paper to take notes."

"Of course," she said. Ten minutes later she had produced

the paper and a pen that read "Will's Feed and Seed" on the side of it. Then she was out the door and off to the store. Wherever that was. I knew there was a town, Olin, about eight miles from her house, but I wasn't sure what direction it was in.

I made a quick call to my mother back home in New Kassel, to make sure the kids were all right, and then got down to business. It wasn't even ten o'clock in the morning and it felt as if half the day were gone.

The pages of the manuscript were yellowed, of course. I'd expected nothing else. They were also pretty brittle. The thing I have noticed about Minnesota is that it is unbelievably dry in the winter and really humid in the summer. Of course, I've never been in the western or northwestern part of the state where it's more prairie, so I'm not sure what their summers are like. But here the constant back and forth of the elements played havoc with this old paper. The ink at one time probably had been blue or black, but it had faded to a sienna brown. Luckily for me, the girl's handwriting was very legible.

> It all began when we moved from Greenup, Minnesota, down to Olin in the autumn of 1857. We lived with cousins of Papa's from Sweden until our house was finished in January of 1858. Olin is a lush and wild place, just miles from the St. Croix River. Greenup had been a bit more harsh and I did not like it so much, except to say that it had been beautiful in the summer.
>
> At first I had been surprised when Papa broke the news to me that we would be moving farther south to a better farm. Mama is not good with English and I knew that

where we were moving to had more of a mixture of Ger-
mans and Finns, and not so many Swedes. Who would
she talk with? And my fear proved correct, for Mama be-
came very withdrawn and stayed to herself, while I became
the woman of the house and went to church and town with
my father and brother.

My little brother, Sven, was as ornery as any little
brother could be. He rarely had a kind word for me and
spent the majority of the days trying to find ways to make
my life more difficult.

The day he killed his first deer by himself was the day
that everything changed. He was but thirteen, and anxious
to prove himself a man. When Sven came home dragging
his deer behind him, Papa acted as though no son in the
world had ever killed a deer. He was so proud and so happy
that he invited some of the neighbors and the parson to
dinner that Sunday after church, to share in my brother's
kill.

Mama made braided bread and paltbrod to go with the
deer. There were twenty people at our house, at least. And
that is where I met Him. The most wonderful, kind, and
amazing man.

I stopped and made some notes. Most works of fiction have
some autobiographical elements in them. People tend to write
what they know, especially their first time out. And even
though the events in the book may never have happened,
things like the character's birthplace might be similar. And the
fact that the book took place in Olin, and this was Olin, made
me think that the book might have more autobiographical in-

formation between the lines. Most likely, whoever wrote it was of Swedish descent. I made a note that read: "What the heck is *paltbrod?*"

I went on to read about the first private meeting between the main character—whose name had, thus far, not been revealed—and the most amazing man on the planet, whom she simply referred to as He or Him with a capital H. The fact that the author never revealed anybody's name in the text, except her little brother's, was beginning to bother me. Would we have *Wuthering Heights* if Heathcliff had remained unnamed? I dare say, no, we would not. I personally think that Heathcliff was an idiot and Cathy was a bitch, but still . . . the names were so important to those nineteenth-century works of fiction. How could this author not give her characters names? I was writing "Names?" on my notepad as Aunt Sissy came back from the store.

"Well," Aunt Sissy said. "How's it going?"

"Pretty good," I said. "I might finish it by tonight, and then I can go and look up everything tomorrow. If that's okay with you."

"Of course," she said. "What do you mean 'look up everything'?"

"Well, I'm making notes of things that I think might be clues to the author's identity as well as landmarks and that sort of thing. I can go and verify these things at the local courthouse, historical society, and so forth."

"I'm amazed," she said. "I didn't expect you to have so many leads so soon."

"Well, they may be nothing," I said. "It depends on how you look at the book. To me, the fact that it takes place here in Olin, and it was found in Olin, must mean that it was written by somebody who lived in Olin—just like the girl in the book. So, I think that tells us that the author probably used some of her own background when writing it."

"I hadn't thought of that," she said. But something made me think that, in fact, she had thought of it. Just the way she cast her eyes around the room as she said it. She pulled out a six-pack of Dr Pepper and my box of party mix and set them down in front of me. Before I could ask for anything else, she got a glass, put a generous amount of ice in it, and set it down next to the soda. "I remember that you hate to drink out of cans or bottles."

"You got that right. I always imagine my spit floating in there."

"Torie, I love you, but you are just too bizarre."

"Thanks," I said. I couldn't help myself, I immediately went back to reading. It was addictive and I wanted to know what happened next. I didn't want to dally and talk with my aunt. I wanted to read.

He touched me everywhere when he kissed me. His hands were on my face, in my hair, on my shoulders, and—

I skipped the next paragraph or so, because I was blushing in front of my aunt. The next paragraph had more of the same. So I skipped another paragraph or two and it had more of the same. His kissing her went on for three bloody pages! And that's all they did as far as I could tell—at that point, anyway. Her clothes remained on, and so did his, but good Lord! None of the Brontës even imagined such a thing, much less wrote

33

about it. Maybe this manuscript would be worth a ton of money as an early example of American erotica.

That wasn't entirely fair of me. I kept reading.

> *The next morning as the sun glistened orange on the freshly fallen snow, I saw a wolf stick its head out of the trees. Her yellow eyes watched me for a long moment without moving, without flinching. I found her the most intoxicating creature I'd ever seen. I went about feeding the chickens, minding my own business to see what the wolf would do. But she only watched with those shimmering eyes that seemed as ancient as the beginning of time.*
>
> *Later that night as I lay in my bed, I heard the wolf's song to the moon. Low and baying at first, then it grew louder and higher in pitch. And then I heard another wolf call to her and join her. And they sang their song of love for nearly a quarter of the night. I found their presence and their music most comforting.*
>
> *Because then I did not think of Him, or the fact that I could not be with Him at that moment.*

And here I thought that being a teenager and boy crazy was a twentieth-century invention. I don't know why, but I wrote the word "wolves" on my notepad, too. Her description of the wolves singing to each other moved me, for some reason. It made me want to know more about them and if they would play a part in her novel later on.

Lunchtime came and went. I kept reading.

Uncle Joe came in, warmed up his food, changed his socks, and ate in silence at the end of the table. He glanced curiously at the manuscript and over at the door that led to the hallway into the main part of the house. But he said nothing. He went back to eating and gave me only a brief nod as he put his shoes on and went back outside.

I noticed his interest, but I did not act as though I wanted to have a conversation, because then I would have had to stop reading.

> Months have passed and I have seen Him only on the briefest occasions. Oh! I think I will die of heartbreak if I do not feel his hands on me again, listen to the beat of his heart, and drink his words of love.

Yuck. I'm sorry, but I just couldn't help but think that this girl needed a hobby. And it struck me then that the author had done such a wonderful job at making her unnamed heroine so believable that I was thinking of her as a real person. So much so that I was trying to think of a hobby for her. That was the best compliment you could give a writer. I kept reading.

> Today there was a festival after church, welcoming the warmth of spring and the fact that long summer days would soon be upon us. Most of the parishioners brought a dish, while the parson supplied the pig.
>
> I stole a moment with Him, in the cemetery, behind the large oak tree. "On many occasions my heart has nearly stopped beating by the merest thought of you," He said to me.
>
> I wept in His hands and He pulled me close to kiss me, but He stopped. He was worried that somebody from the festival would see us. But before He left, He took my

hands and cupped them with His own. "As I stand on sacred ground, I vow to thee that we will be together. Soon. And if you love me as you have professed all these long winter months, then say that you will be my wife."

I was so overcome with joy that I sobbed the answer in His ear. "Yes, my love. Yes."

And then He was gone. And it was another week before I would see Him again.

And on that meeting we joined. We lay together on a bed of hay, under the stars. Such joy I have never known. Such oneness with another . . .

I skipped a few paragraphs because she went into some pretty explicit detail of what all had happened, and I felt like a Peeping Tom.

When it was over, He lay still and quiet on top of me, as if He had died. And as I looked up at the sky, I felt as if we were being watched. My eyes fell to the line of trees. Those golden eyes of the wolf shimmered off of the moonlight and I saw her, crouched there by the pine tree that grows crooked on the edge of the woods.

The wolf did not move, and neither did I, but an understanding had passed between us. We are not so different, she and I. Making music under the moonlight with the love of my life. After a moment, she ran across the field and behind the house.

And I said farewell to my lover for the night.

When He was gone and I was alone in my bed, listening to the silence of the night and the creaks of the house, I thought of Him and found it difficult to breathe.

*Somewhere in the night, the wolf found her mate, and
they sang their song of love. How jealous I was of her.
That she could be with hers, and I could not.*

Aunt Sissy came in to cook dinner, and I looked up from
my manuscript, glassy-eyed and nursing a screaming headache.
"Do I look as bad as I feel?"

"You've been reading for about six hours straight," she said.
"You're entitled to look like hell."

"Thanks."

She shrugged. "Why don't you stop until after dinner?" she
said.

"To be honest, I don't know if I can finish this today," I
said, flipping through the remaining stack of papers. "I'm about
halfway."

She shrugged.

"I've got quite a bit to go on. I can start researching it
tomorrow just the same," I said.

"Good," she said.

"I have the feeling that this doesn't end well. Does it?"

"I wouldn't know," she said. "It has no ending."

"Okay, whatever. But I think you know what I mean," I
said.

"You like chicken?"

"Yes," I said.

"Good, I'm going to have Joe barbecue some chicken, and
I'm going to make all the trimmings. You like corn on the cob?"

"Oh, do I," I said and stretched. "When are the guys due
back?"

"Well, I told the big one that dinner would be at six, so I
expect they'll be back in about an hour," she said.

I chuckled at that. "All right. I'm going to take a walk," I said. "I've been sitting in one position for hours. I need to stretch."

"Okay," she said. "Just wear a jacket. It's getting chilly out there. Think we might get rain tomorrow."

I grabbed my jacket and headed out to the front porch. The lilacs smelled so good that I just stood on the concrete steps breathing as deeply as I could for about five minutes. I ran my hand across the bushes as I headed around the side of the house and out to the stables. I stopped and petted the horses for a few minutes and waved at Uncle Joe, who looked like he was building some sort of shelter out in the field for the animals.

I walked aimlessly for the longest time and then began walking west, away from Aunt Sissy's house. I only know this because that was the direction that the sun was headed. I looked back at the house, and it was maybe two hundred feet away. I stretched again and shook my head trying to clear the cobwebs. But it didn't work very well. The Swedish girl's words kept ringing through my head. I found that the thoughts in my mind were forming in the rhythm of her sentences.

And then I saw it. I stopped frozen in my tracks, the hair rising on the back of my neck. At the edge of the woods was a pine tree. It grew straight for about two feet and then the trunk bowed to the left for another two feet and then grew straight again: *the pine tree that grows crooked on the edge of the woods . . .*

It couldn't be. There was no way. I walked over to it and stopped when I got about a hundred yards from it. I looked up and down the row of trees. It was the only crooked pine tree that I could see.

I looked back at the house and hugged myself close. Could

this be the crooked pine tree that the girl had written about? But then that would mean that this land was the backdrop for her novel, too. Not just the town of Olin. Which meant whoever wrote it had lived here.

Five

It's just a crooked pine tree, I told myself. There must be hundreds of crooked pine trees in Minnesota. Right?

Right. Hundreds of them. I'm not sure how long I stood there and stared at that stupid pine tree, with its crooked trunk situated perfectly on the edge of the woods. Voices from the past swirled around in my head, and I just couldn't shake the feeling that everything had just changed. Rudy's voice brought me back to the twenty-first century, the here and now. I turned around in time to see him walking up behind me. The smile on his face was unmistakable.

He had caught a fish.

"You shoulda seen it, honey. It almost got away . . ." The smile faded from his face when he saw me. "What's wrong?"

"What do you mean, what's wrong?" I asked.

"You've got that look in your eyes."

"What look?"

"That look that says I'm going to lose a lot of sleep."

"Oh, please," I said. I headed back toward Aunt Sissy's house.

"I'm telling you, you were standing there working your lower lip between your thumb and finger . . . like, like you do when you're onto something."

I laughed. "You're so silly."

"Do not call me silly. I might be a lot of things, but I am not silly."

"Just hearing you say it makes you sound silly," I said.

"D-did you see the way you did that?" he asked, walking along beside me.

"Did what?"

"Turned it on me. This conversation was a study of your behavior, not mine. And you just whipped it around and now I'm defending myself," he said, snapping his fingers. "How do you do that?"

"Practice, I guess."

"Well, stop it. Now, what was that look back there for?"

"I've discovered why Aunt Sissy asked me to come up," I said. "Other than the fact that she wanted to see me and other than to give you a chance at fishing."

"What?" he asked. "What is it? Is it bad? You look like it's bad."

"Well, you know how she said she wanted some help with something?"

He nodded.

"She wants me to find out who wrote a novel that takes place like a hundred and fifty years ago."

"Oh, is that all? Just go to the library. They have all sorts of reference books about those sorts of things," he said.

"It was never published," I said.

"Oh," he said. Then he stopped and turned to me. "Oh."

"Yeah. It was left here on the property when they moved in and she wants me to find out who wrote it," I said. "So, I'm going to be spending a lot of time reading and a lot of time behind microfilm readers, I suspect."

"But nobody's been killed, kidnapped, shysted, or shanghaied. Right?"

I punched him in the arm. "Right. But it's never to late for you to succumb to an uncertain demise."

He rubbed his arm. "All right," he said. "I get the picture. Now, can I tell you my fish story?"

"Of course," I said.

"Oh, man, it was just amazing . . . Why were you staring into the woods? Just now."

"It's nothing," I said. "Go ahead, tell me your fish story."

And so all the way back to Aunt Sissy's house he dazzled me with his fish story and how the little sucker almost got away—whatever it was, and when we made it to the front porch and he showed me his fish . . . well, it was just a fish. It was dead. It was harmless, and it didn't look all that big. Maybe it had just been a clever fish. Either way, I was happy for Rudy that even though Colin caught three more fish than he had, he had caught the biggest. That was important.

"Does Aunt Sissy know that her front porch is now the home to dead fish?" I asked.

He put his hands in his pockets. "Well, sure. I guess."

"Rudy O'Shea, you get those dead fish off of my front porch and out into the shed!" Aunt Sissy had appeared in the doorway like magic, out of the mists of her living room, with a giant fork in her hand and a scowl that would scare even the bravest of hearts. At that moment she reminded me of my boss,

Sylvia. Sylvia, although twenty-plus years older than my Aunt Sissy, could just appear out of nowhere and bark commands that everybody seemed to follow. Even when you weren't sure why.

I just smiled.

"I spent years getting these lilacs to grow, and they only bloom a few weeks, and I want to smell them, not your dead fish. Next time I'm just going to invite Torie."

"Yes, ma'am," he said.

"Now!" she exclaimed and pointed off in the direction of the shed with her giant fork.

"Of course," he said.

"You need some help with dinner, Aunt Sissy?" I asked.

"Yes, you can shuck corn and slice tomatoes."

Which I did, while Rudy and Colin removed their fish to the shed and began to clean them. When they were finished, they both snuck inside through the front door and went upstairs to take their showers. I set the table, and all the while Aunt Sissy talked about her beloved cherry trees in the backyard. I couldn't take it anymore. I didn't want to hear about another cherry tree or how the birds loved to eat the cherries or how many bushels they yielded or canned or whatever. I wanted to know about something else.

"Did you find the crooked pine?" I asked.

She was taking the baked beans out of the oven and sort of stopped midway. Obviously she had found the crooked pine. She stood up the rest of the way and set the baked beans on a hot plate. "What do you mean?"

"Oh, come on. Don't play games," I said. "You found the crooked pine. The one she talks about in the novel."

"We can't talk about this during dinner," she said.

"Okay," I said. I didn't ask why. I assumed it had something to do with Uncle Joe. Either she didn't want him to know, or he already knew and was upset by her obsession with it. But he had seen me reading the manuscript earlier at lunch and he hadn't asked any questions. So I was assuming that he knew about it already and she just didn't want to aggravate a sore spot between them. "But it's not dinnertime, yet."

She looked around quickly. "Okay, yes. The tree is the thing that really got me going. I just couldn't stop thinking about it after that. When I saw that crooked pine, I got goose bumps all down me and it just made it seem . . . real."

With that, Uncle Joe came in with the chicken on a big red, white, and blue platter. "Mmm, baked beans smell good," he said.

"So does the chicken," I said.

Aunt Sissy and I exchanged a knowing glance and just shut up. Colin came barreling downstairs within seconds of Uncle Joe coming in the door, and Rudy followed right on his heels.

Dinner was delicious and the talk around the table was mostly of Rudy and Colin's adventures on the boat. "I'm all for going back out on the same lake tomorrow," Colin said. "The fishing was good and the lake itself was just beautiful."

"Yes," Uncle Joe said. "Olin Lake was once described by the early settlers as the sapphire of the prairie. Of course, this isn't technically prairie right here. We're sort of on the edge of the prairie and the edge of the forest. Nevertheless, the lake was one of the things that even the earliest settlers recognized as an asset to their community. I think the historical society even has some photographs of sailboats and such out on the lake around the turn of the century," he said, and took a bite of tomato.

"Oooh, neat," I said. "Maybe Aunt Sissy and I can go to the historical society tomorrow and see them."

"That would be right up your alley, that's for certain," Uncle Joe said.

"Hey, on the way back from fishing, Colin and I saw a bunch of people gathered up on the road. I just thought a deer had been hit by a car, but everybody seemed to be pretty interested in it, so it can't have been roadkill," Rudy said.

Uncle Joe swallowed. "Yeah, one of the farmers over in the valley lost one of his pigs."

"Lost it?" I asked.

"Predator carried it off. They found what was left of it by the road," Uncle Joe said.

"Don't they have llamas?" I asked.

"As a matter of fact, they do," Aunt Sissy said.

"A llama isn't going to work against a bear," Uncle Joe said.

"You think it was a bear?" I asked. "You think a bear carried off a pig in broad daylight?"

"Well, I'm sure it wasn't broad daylight," he said. "And I'm not saying it was a bear. I'm just saying that a llama isn't going to be able to fight off everything. They're mostly good for coyotes."

"Great," I said.

"There's no bear," Rudy said. "Don't worry about it."

"It was a little pig," Colin said.

"A little pig? What has that got to do with it?" I asked.

"Meaning that it was probably something little that killed it."

"Oh, like a little bear?" I said.

He rolled his eyes.

"So what else do you have of historical interest in this town?" Colin asked. Colin could have cared less about historical things, but he knew I did. He was trying to get the subject away from bears. It was sort of sweet. Like he was actually worried about me being afraid.

Uncle Joe shrugged. "Well, there's the historical society. There's a little house that is set up like a frontier house. You can tour it. Gives you an idea of what life was like in the olden days. And then, we have a festival coming up at the Lutheran church," he said. "They sell jams and apple butter and pies and things like that. They have wood carving and a strongman competition."

"When is that?" I asked.

"I believe it's this week. They do it every spring. From what I understand they've done it every spring since the church was built," he said.

"Oh, that sounds like fun," I said.

"Yeah," Colin said. "I'd love to see the strongman competition."

"That will probably be on the weekend," Aunt Sissy said. "They save those big events like that for when people are off from work."

"Sounds like I've got a few things to check out," I said. "I'm not opposed to taking home a couple of jars of apple butter."

"And where are you going to put it?" Colin asked. "We were cramped in the car as it was."

"I'm sure if I pack it well enough, it can go in the back of the truck. Or if nothing else, I'll put it under the seat," I said. "Mom would be very hurt if I came back without some apple butter or blackberry jam."

Colin turned to Rudy. "We have to get in all the fishing we can before the weekend," he said. "I want to see the strongman competition."

"Okay," Rudy said. "Torie, what are you doing tomorrow?"

I looked at Aunt Sissy, whose expression did not change. "I think I'm going to start at the historical society," I said. "That sounds interesting."

Six

The next morning I awoke feeling that I hadn't slept at all. I'm not sure if it was the travel just catching up with me or what. I don't sleep well in other people's homes anyway, and every time I woke up, I found myself thinking about the Swedish girl and the anonymous novel. Then I'd doze off and wake up an hour later, still thinking about them.

Breakfast was at six in the morning, sharp. Aunt Sissy never varied breakfast or lunch times, and dinner only on special occasions. So I found myself scarfing down scrambled eggs and sliced tomatoes with grit still in my eyes and my hair standing on end. Afterward, I helped Uncle Joe clean out the stables—a thrill a minute, I'll tell you—and then took a shower. Nothing like horse crap imbedding itself in your nasal cavity to put you in a great mood. By the time I'd finished my chores, I felt like Laura Ingalls, waiting for Aunt Sissy at the foot of her steps to take us into town.

And I was wondering, why wasn't Rudy or Colin having to shovel horse crap?

"You ready?" she asked.

"Oh, yes," I said. "I'm actually looking forward to it."

"Ha," she said. "Be right back."

She disappeared into the garage and then came back sitting behind the wheel of a beat-up pickup truck that spit and sputtered. She rolled the window down. "Get in. This is your limo for the day."

I had to hike my pants leg to get up in the darn thing. It seemed as if the floorboard was four feet off the ground. The leather in the seat was ripped and the dash still had one of those push-button radios in it. The truck was evidently built before the invention of shock absorbers, and with every little rock, hole, or bump that Aunt Sissy drove over, I went up in the air—with plenty of hang time—and flopped back down on the seat. Then I'd hear *squeegee, squeegee, squeegee.* It was a veritable symphony of springs, pings, and squeegees all the way to town.

Aunt Sissy sang at the top of her lungs to the country station that was on the radio. A song about a windshield and a bug. I just looked out the window at all the trees and smiled to myself, wondering why I hadn't had the brains to think up a song about a windshield and a bug. Her voice, strangely enough, seemed to fit right in with all the noise.

Town was about ten minutes away. Olin was sort of like New Kassel, in the sense that it was a one-horse town, if you know what I mean. There was a grocery store that doubled as a post office, a drugstore, a jail, a bar, about twelve streets of houses, a lake—of course, two churches, each with a cemetery—a historical society, and "the homestead" museum. I saw a deli when we first came in, but otherwise no restaurants or hotels. "Where's the school?" I asked Aunt Sissy.

"Oh, they bus the kids over to Cedar Springs," she said. "All the kids from this half of the county go to the same school. There wouldn't be enough kids to fill up individual ones in each town."

Well, at least New Kassel had its own school, a few restaurants, and a bed-and-breakfast. "Oh," I said.

Aunt Sissy waved at a woman on the street and she waved back. Neighborliness was something I could relate to. I would bet that everybody here knew everybody else. Aunt Sissy and Uncle Joe were probably the outsiders. "Did you have trouble when you moved here?" I asked.

"How do you mean?"

"About being accepted."

"Oh, that," she said, and waved. "At first people were real friendly, but it was on the surface. You know? Nobody was rude to us, but we got left out of a lot of things. Guess it was about three years ago when people finally realized that we weren't strangers anymore," she said. She shifted gears. "But I've never met nicer people."

"Well, that's good," I said. If there was one thing I knew, it was that small towns could be terribly cliquish.

She pulled the truck in front of a perfectly square, drab, gray building that had a hand-painted sign that read OLIN HISTORICAL SOCIETY. PLEASE CALL BEFORE COMING.

"Please call?"

"It's all volunteer," she explained. "Sometimes Roberta doesn't feel like coming in."

"Did we call ahead?"

"No need to."

"Why?" I asked, amazed at her blatant lack of respect for proper procedure.

"Because on Mondays Roberta's husband is off from work. She's always here on Mondays."

"Oh," I said.

We walked in the building to find a woman sitting behind a small student-sized desk. She was about forty and had long dark hair. She looked up from what she was reading. "Hey, Sissy. What's up?"

"This is my niece, Torie O'Shea," she said. "I told you she might be coming up."

"Oh," the woman said, as if that explained it all. "The genealogist."

"Hi," I said, and waved.

"My name's Roberta Flagg," she said.

"Fleg?" I asked, and looked at my aunt.

"F-l-a-g-g," she said. "You'll notice that a bag is a beg up here, too."

"Oh," I said. "Nice to meet you."

"My pleasure," she said. She gave a sweeping motion to the room around her. "Well, this is it."

I smiled. What was I supposed to do? The room had depressing brown paneling and the floor was concrete that had been painted tan. Filing cabinets filled one wall, and several cases of books lined the wall behind her desk. Glass cases with various memorabilia made a U shape in the middle of the room. Several photographs hung crookedly on the walls. And in a vain attempt to dress up the place, somebody had placed potted plants by windows that sported bright pink curtains. I couldn't help but step over and look at the photographs.

"I hear you're from a small town, too," Roberta said.

"Yes, I am," I said.

"And you work for the historical society?"

"Yes," I said, studying a photograph closely. It seemed as though I had found the photographs Uncle Joe had referred to. There were three sailboats out on Olin Lake, with men in suits and women with long beautiful dresses and parasols. I would guess the photograph was taken about 1905.

"So what's your historical society like?" Roberta asked.

Before I had the chance to answer, Aunt Sissy flew into a colorful description of the Gaheimer House and the gowns that I give the tours in and ended with an even more colorful description of my boss, Sylvia Pershing, and her sister, Wilma.

"Oh, Aunt Sissy, I forgot to tell you that Wilma died."

"No," she said.

"Yes."

"Well, don't that beat all. I honestly thought she and Sylvia were going to be the first immortal human beings," she said.

"Well, Sylvia's still kicking. I think it would take a train to stop her."

"Well, nevertheless," Aunt Sissy went on, "the Pershings were still a pair of great old ladies."

Roberta put her hand on her hip. "I'm so jealous," she said. "Why?"

"You work in a big beautiful house with antiques and you have authentic reproduction dresses? I get four walls, my sweat outfits, and Hank the wandering can collector for company."

"Olin isn't a tourist town," I said. "Otherwise, you'd probably have better facilities, too. In New Kassel, that's all we do. We survive and prosper on tourists, so we cater to that."

"Well, what can I help you find?" she asked.

I pulled out my notebook, which I had shoved down in the

back flap of my purse. I scanned my notes and then put it back. "You don't have a microfilm reader here, so I'm assuming this is not where you keep things like census records."

"I've got a few in book form that some other volunteers and I transcribed one year. What year are you looking for?"

"I'm thinking 1860."

"Yes, that's one of the ones we have in book form," she said. She pulled it off of a shelf behind her desk and handed it to me. "Anything else?"

"Where would I get ahold of the census records for Greenup?"

"At the library."

I nodded to Aunt Sissy. We needed to go to the library, then, if for nothing else than to get a look at the 1850 census for Greenup. "What about church records? I noticed that you've got two churches in town. Do you have their records here or are they at the churches?"

"They are at the individual churches. I think they've been copied by the Latter Day Saints Library, so you can probably find them on-line now. Or at your local LDS Library. But since you're here, I would just go over to the church and ask to see their records," she said.

"Great."

"Which church do you need?"

"I don't know. What kind of churches are they? I saw a Lutheran one when we came in."

"Yes, the other one is Catholic."

"Mmmm, I doubt that they were Catholic."

"Why's that?" Aunt Sissy asked.

"She called him a parson in the book. I think even in 1858 if she were Catholic, she would have referred to him as Father or as a priest. I don't think she would have called him a parson. So I'm thinking the Lutheran church would be our best bet. But if I come up empty, I'll still check out the Catholic church," I said.

"The office at the Lutheran church is open from about ten in the morning to four in the afternoon," Roberta said.

"Great," I said. "Oh, and land records. I need to find out who owned a specific lot of land."

"Do you know when it was bought?" she asked.

"I want to know who owned Aunt Sissy's land before she did."

"Oh, that's easy," Roberta said. "The Olsons owned it."

"No, I mean, all the way back."

She handed me a stack of books. "The land records we have transcribed," she said. Roberta was proud of herself, smiling at my Aunt Sissy, happy that she could assist with my hunt. That's the thing about us historians and genealogists. We get almost as much satisfaction helping others with their hunts as we do when we're solving our own mysteries.

I looked around the room and there were no other chairs, so I just opened the books on one of the glass cases and began scanning them. Roberta was correct: Kevin Olson and his wife, Belinda, had owned the property before my aunt.

"So, you're going to try to find the authoress of the novel?" Roberta asked.

I looked at her quickly and then at my aunt. "You know about it?" I asked.

"Of course," Roberta said. "Sissy tried to figure it out herself, before calling you. She sort of enlisted all of our help."

"Who's all?" I asked, and flipped a page.

"Everybody in our quilting bee and prayer group," she said.

"Which is one and the same. We all get together and pray that our stitches hold."

I laughed, which was what I was supposed to do, and flipped another page.

"I'm the youngest one in the group," Roberta said. "Why don't you come to our next meeting? It'd be nice to have somebody my own age in the group. I'm forty-one, and the next closest is . . . Diane. She's what, about fifty?"

Aunt Sissy nodded. "About that."

I did not slap the woman across the face for suggesting that I was forty-one. I was pushing forty, but I wasn't there yet. Instead, I smiled and flipped another page, accepting the fact that I was no longer a spring chicken. It wasn't the fact that I was not a spring chicken that bothered me. It was the fact that everybody else knew I was not a spring chicken. People treat you differently when you're over thirty, and once you hit forty, it's as if everybody just counts you out. Of course, revenge would be mine, because everybody's going to get there, eventually. Probably the same thing that everyone older than me was thinking, too.

"I'm not a very good quilter," I said.

"Well, you don't have to quilt," Roberta said.

"I'm not a very good prayer, either."

"Oh, nonsense."

"No, seriously. I always think my prayers sound so stupid. So I don't say them out loud if I don't have to."

Roberta and Sissy both laughed. I was being serious.

I stopped and looked at the names on the page. I had found the next entry to the land that was now my aunt Sissy's. The Olsons had bought it from . . . the Hujinaks. "Hujinak?"

"Yes," Roberta said. "What about them?"

"What kind of name is that?"

"Yugoslavian, most likely. There's a large population of Slavs up on the range. They came in around 1900 to 1915 and worked in the iron-ore mines."

"Oh," I said. I had no idea what she was talking about. "The range?"

"The great Mesabi," she said.

She said it with such matter-of-factness that I dared not tell her I still didn't know what she was talking about.

"Anyway, some of them, if they had the money, would move farther south or west, either to be farmers or loggers. Depending on which area they moved to. This area was once a haven for loggers. All that white pine. But that's all gone now," Roberta said.

"In other words, this Hujinak family came down from the range to be loggers or farmers?"

"Most likely," she said. "You can ask them. Good Lord, I think there were thirteen or fourteen kids in that family. Most of them are still in the area. The mayor is one of them."

"Yeah," Aunt Sissy said. "Mayor Tom. I never call him Mayor Hujinak. I forgot that was his last name."

"Everybody calls him Mayor Tom," Roberta said. "He goes to St. Catherine's, owns a farm out on J highway. His daughter is a riding champion."

"Riding champion?"

"Horses."

"Oh," I said. I looked at Aunt Sissy. "You think I could talk with him sometime this week?"

"I don't see why not. Friendliest guy I've ever met," Aunt Sissy said.

"Is the Lutheran church the church that you go to, Aunt Sissy?"

"Yes," she said.

"Good," I said. "Is there a church historian or somebody that I could talk to?"

"Mmmm, Lisa. She could probably help you the most. Or even Diane."

I flipped a few more pages and put that book away. I would need the land records prior to 1930. "Where's the courthouse?" I asked.

"Oh, over in Cedar Springs," Roberta said.

I flipped through the pages of the next book until I found the Hujinak name. I love unusual names, because they are the easiest to trace. I felt like weeping for people who had to trace names like Jones or Johnson. Or Schmidt! Ugh. Or names that have other uses outside of last names. Like Acre, Justice, or Brown. Those are hard, too. Especially on the Internet. Put in the name Acre, and you'll get all of these hits from people posting land that they want to sell. So a name like Hujinak is a godsend to a genealogist.

"Okay," I said and got out my paper. "Hujinaks bought the land in 1928 from . . . Wendell Reed."

"Don't recognize that name," Roberta said.

"I wonder why the land stayed vacant so long," I said.

"What do you mean?" Roberta asked.

"Aunt Sissy said that before the Olsons bought the land it had stood vacant for a long time. The Hujinaks owned it the whole time. So why didn't anybody live in it?"

"I think Mr. Hujinak died in the late fifties, and his wife went to live with one of the kids and died in the early sixties. I never met her, but I remember my mother talking about her. I don't know why it took them so long to sell it."

"Well, at any rate, they bought it in 1928."

"Just before the crash," Aunt Sissy said.

"Yes, I noticed that," I said. "A year later, they were most likely sweating bullets. Probably thought they were going to lose their farm."

I kept searching through the records and about ten minutes later found where Wendell Reed had bought the land in 1910. He had bought it from somebody with the last name Hendrickson. Twenty minutes later I had found the entry for the Hendricksons, who had bought the land in 1878. "Hey, eighteen seventy-eight," I said.

Aunt Sissy perked up and looked over my shoulder. "Who owned it?"

"Uh . . . Roy Hendrickson bought it in 1878. Isn't that when you said a new house was built?"

"Yes," she said. "He must have been the one who built it."

"Who told you that was the year a new house was built?"

"Oh, um, the Olsons told me."

"They must have researched it some themselves," I said.

"What else did you find?" Roberta asked.

"Well, the Hendricksons bought it from a James Rogers in 1878, who bought it in 1861," I said. My stomach sort of flip-flopped. If our Swedish girl had moved into the house in 1858 and somebody else bought it in 1861, that meant that her family hadn't lived there very long. That gave me a most disturbing feeling. I flipped more pages, more pages, and then I traced the lines with my finger until I found it. "Here it is. Karl Bloomquist."

Nobody said anything for a minute. We just sort of let the name hang in the air. "Karl Bloomquist bought the land in 1857. That's right. Because in the novel, she says they lived with a cousin while the house was being built. They moved into the house in 1858."

"That's weird," Roberta said.

"Why? What's weird?"

"Isn't it strange that not one of those people willed their land to any of their offspring? I mean, how many other tracts of land would be sold time after time and never pass from father to son?"

"That is pretty unusual," I said. "Now that you mention it."

All three of us were quiet a minute. I tapped Roberta on the shoulder. "Hey, you're all right, Roberta."

"Thanks," she said. "Anytime."

"Oh, don't make that offer," I warned.

"Why not?"

"Because I'll take you up on it," I said and smiled. "And you may regret it later."

"Now what?" Aunt Sissy asked.

"Well, next on the list is the census. We know for sure that the Bloomquists owned the land in 1860 when the census was taken. So, now we need to find out if the Bloomquists had a son named Sven and a daughter."

"And whoever the daughter is, she's the author of the book?" Aunt Sissy asked.

"It seems too easy," I said. "But I guess so."

"I can't believe it," Aunt Sissy said.

"But I'm no closer to finding the ending of the book."

"The ending of the book?" Roberta asked.

"Yes, the novel has no ending. Aunt Sissy thinks I'm going to be able to find the end of the story by finding the author. I think she probably got bored and just didn't finish it," I said.

"You haven't finished reading it yet," Aunt Sissy said. "There is no way that she could have just not finished the novel."

"Yes, something I must remedy tonight," I said, thinking about the pages waiting to be read. "Guess I should open this census book and find our novelist."

"I can't stand the wait," Roberta said. "Open the darned book."

"Did you index it?" I asked.

"Yes."

I flipped to the index in the back and found the name Bloomquist. I found Karl and flipped to the page that he was listed for. "This can't be right."

"What?" Aunt Sissy asked.

"Well, there are no Bloomquists on this page."

"What do you mean?" Roberta asked.

I scanned the heads of households and none of them had the last name Bloomquist. Then it occurred to me. This was 1860; what if the fire had already occurred? Then the Bloomquists wouldn't have had any place to live. They would be staying with somebody else. I scanned each household and found: Bloomquist, Karl. Age 43. White. Male. Born in Sweden. Occupation was laborer. Meaning that he was most likely a farmer but as a guest in somebody else's home. A laborer.

"Here he is," I said.

"Who is he living with?" Roberta asked.

"What do you mean?" Aunt Sissy asked.

"If he's in the index, but he's not a head of household, that means he's staying with another family."

"Well, who is it?" Roberta asked.

"Johann Hagglund." Most likely, at one time, the last name would have had the two little dots over the *a*, but a few years on the frontier and you just got the spelling that the census taker felt like giving you.

"By himself? Where's his family?"

"His son, Sven, is the only one listed with him," I said. I couldn't believe it. We were that close to finding out who the author of the book was and then, boom, it was gone. The disappointment was indescribable. All three of us sighed.

"Well, fiddlesticks," Roberta declared.

I just looked at her. Only my grandmother says fiddlesticks.

"Now what?" Aunt Sissy said.

"Now I check the church records. We know they were here."

"Yes, but if she wasn't baptized or married or didn't die during that time, she's not going to be listed," Roberta said.

I didn't say anything. Aunt Sissy knew what I was thinking. There was a reason that the Bloomquists were not in their home. Most likely it was the fire. And if the fire was truth, not just a myth, then the possibility of the Swedish girl meeting her demise in the cellar could be the truth, too. The fact that neither she nor her mother was listed with the father and the brother just made that possibility all that more likely.

Roberta realized what we were thinking. "Wait. Now wait, I know what you're thinking. But couldn't she be living with somebody else? Maybe the Hagglund family didn't have room for everybody, so they had to split up."

I checked the index for more Bloomquists, but there were none.

"Not unless she and the mother changed their last names or moved out of the state."

"Well, spit fire," Aunt Sissy said.

I was going to have to teach these people how to curse.

"Come on. I think the church records are our best bet."

Seven

It was nearly noon before we made it over to the church. My stomach rumbled as if it hadn't been fed in days. But I suppose that's what happens when you eat breakfast before the sun comes up. I said nothing and just hoped that Aunt Sissy would hear my stomach growling and suggest lunch. It was a crisp day and I could smell the oxygen heavy in the air. The sun was golden yellow, everything was in early bloom, and it was on days like this that you thought, it can't get much better than this.

The Olin Lutheran Church was a white clapboard building, oblong, with a steeple. A newer part of the building sat off to the left-hand side—the office, I presumed. The cemetery began about two hundred yards from the back of the church, and there was a large field off to the right with picnic benches and lots of trees. A cluster of birch trees sat almost perfectly in the center of the field. Funny, at that moment I thought that I could have sat there beneath those trees all day.

I grudgingly went inside the office part of the church, following closely behind Aunt Sissy. The office seemed dark, since we'd just left the brilliant sunshine just seconds before. "Well, Sissy. How are you?" I heard a voice say.

"I'm fine. Lisa, this is my niece, Torie."

"Hi, I've heard so much about you."

"She's my brother's daughter," she said. "Of course, we just all recently found out he has two daughters."

Lisa, a woman of about twenty-five years with bobbed blond hair, raised her eyebrows at that remark.

"Very sweet girl," Aunt Sissy said.

"Well, are you just sightseeing?" Lisa asked.

"No, actually," Aunt Sissy said. "We're here to see the records."

Lisa raised her eyebrows again. "Records?"

I interjected, finally. "We were wondering if we could see the baptism, marriage, and death records that you may have on file here?"

"For what year?"

"Oh, it would be like . . . well, when do your records start?"

"The church was built in 1854. Our records start in 1854."

"Well, then, I guess, give me the records for 1854 to about 1861," I said.

"Sure," she said. "Come on."

She led us to the back of the office and to a door that connected with the church. It also connected to another door that opened into the basement. Lisa flipped on the light. "You have to forgive us, but we don't have a whole lot of room."

I've seen worse basements. This one was dry, with concrete walls and that green plastic turf on the floor for carpeting. The whole room was nothing but filing cabinets. There was a funny smell to the room, even though it seemed to be perfectly dry. Maybe it was just the smell that all basements have, regardless. Except my mother-in-law's. Hers smelled like Febreze.

Lisa opened up the top drawer on the first filing cabinet. "Here you go." Inside were big leather books. One was marked: Marriages 1854–1875 A–M. I found the N–Z book right below it. Below that was births and baptisms. The last one was deaths. "Let me know if you need anything else."

"All right," I said. Lisa walked back up the basement steps to her office and I let out a deep breath. "I don't even know her name to look up a death record."

"Can't you just look under Bloomquist?"

"Well, yeah. But . . . that doesn't mean it will be the same person who wrote the novel. Unless . . ."

"Unless what?"

"Unless it actually gives her father's name," I said. "All I can do is look."

I pulled out the death registry and scanned the pages. Now, I'm not sure what the official date in Minnesota is, but in most states nobody had to report a birth or a death prior to 1910. In West Virginia, it's 1917. Therefore, any reports of births or deaths prior to about 1910 in this country were strictly voluntary. There were a lot more reported to the local parishes than one realizes. But fire on the frontier was a serious problem, due to the fact that most of the churches were built out of wood, and so a lot of the records were lost. Plus, trying to find the church that your ancestor attended can be a real problem. And sometimes churches just fell by the wayside or were incorporated into another church, so you never know where your ancestor's records will end up.

The point to all this is that as I stood there holding that

death registry in my hands, I knew that even if the girl I was looking for had died in this county, between 1854 and 1875, I would only find the record in this book if her parents had voluntarily reported her death. I opened the book and held my breath as I scanned the names. They were not listed alphabetically, but rather by year. Most likely, the names had just been written in this book as the deaths were reported. So I had to read every name.

There it was. Bloomquist, Brigitta, age thirty-nine. Died on the third of June 1859.

"That can't be her. She's too old. That has to be her mother," I said.

"What did she die of?"

"It says . . . it says . . . she died in a fire. Person reporting her death was her son, Sven. And then it gives her place of birth and who her parents were," I said, amazed. "You go, Sven."

"What does that mean?"

"I mean, for as young as he was, Sven knew enough about his mother to put down her place of birth and her parents' names. I have an ancestor who didn't even know his own father's name."

"How could he not know his own father's name?"

"Evidently his father died when he was really young and his mother never told him his name. So when he got married and they asked him for his parents' names, he said, 'Father, unknown.' "

"Either that or his mother didn't know who his father was either."

"Yeah, I considered that."

"So, the girl. Is she in here or is it just her mother?" Aunt Sissy asked.

"I'm looking," I said. "Oh, my God."

"What?"

"She's here," I said. Goose bumps broke out along the backs of my arms and down my legs. "Bloomquist, Anna. Age seventeen years, nine months, and ten days. Cause of death is fire. Oh, God."

"What?"

"It says she lingered for five days. She died on the eighth of June 1859. Parents were Brigitta and Karl. Person reporting the death was her brother, Sven."

"I don't know if I'm happy that we found her or not," Aunt Sissy said.

"Yeah," I said. I stood there for a minute taking it all in. It was true. Aunt Sissy's rumor was actually true. But as with all rumors, it wasn't exactly the same. The girl had not died in the fire, the mother had. The girl, Anna Bloomquist, had lingered for five days and died after the fire. I could only assume that if she had indeed fled to the cellar, as the rumor went, she had died of a fatal dose of smoke inhalation.

The next name on the page caught my eye. The name Bloomquist, once again.

Bloomquist, Emelie, age two months. Cause of death, fire. Parents were Anna Bloomquist and father unknown. Informant: Sven Bloomquist, uncle. "Oh, no," I said. I covered my mouth and fought back tears.

"What?" Aunt Sissy asked.

"She had a baby."

"What?" The look of horror spread across my aunt's face.

"Right here," I said. "The baby died with her. She had a baby."

"No," Aunt Sissy whispered.

"I can only assume, since its last name was Bloomquist and she was at her father's house, that she was unwed. That means . . . that means Anna and her lover never married."

"No," Aunt Sissy said. "Oh, why did I have you look? I wish I didn't know."

We both just stood there, completely numb. And then it hit me. She never finished the novel because it wasn't fiction. It was a diary. She never finished it because her death was the ending. "Aunt Sissy," I said. "I need to finish reading what's written."

"Okay."

"Because I don't think it's fiction at all. I think it was a diary."

Aunt Sissy nodded her head. "I've always thought so. Ever since I found the crooked tree."

I looked at her for a moment and wondered why on earth then she had presented that manuscript to me as a work of fiction. That was what she had called it. She had called it a novel. I couldn't be angry with her. Maybe she thought that if she told me it was a diary I wouldn't investigate it. That I would feel weird reading it. Well, she didn't know me very well, if that's what she thought. I am the nosiest person in the world and would have read it without a second thought. I might have read it with a little more caution, though.

I copied all the information down. "Damn," I said, and shut the book.

"Why are you writing this stuff down? We've found it," Aunt Sissy said. "We found what we were looking for. And now I even know how the story ended."

"I know," I said. "Just habit, I guess."

We both walked up the steps having lost all of the bounce

and vigor that we had had when we came in. Which was silly. We had come here looking for the girl's death record, and then, when we found it, we wished we hadn't.

"Did you find what you needed?" Lisa asked.

"Yes," I said.

"Yeah, thanks," Aunt Sissy said.

With that we both walked out into the gorgeous sunshine and perfectly blissful spring air, feeling . . . feeling . . . well, feeling like we knew something we shouldn't.

"I'm hungry," Aunt Sissy said. "Are you?"

"Starved."

"Good, we're going over to the Pancake Palace."

"Where's that?"

"It's on the way to Cedar Springs. I'm gonna eat until I puke," she said.

"Yeah, me, too."

Eight

The Pancake Palace had a giant ten-foot stack of pancakes on its roof to alert passersby on Highway 35 that it was there. I sat in a booth with my much smaller stack of pancakes looming in front of me. "I think my eyes were bigger than my belly," I said.

"Give it your best shot," Aunt Sissy said.

"Oh, I will," I said.

Pancakes in the middle of the day are sort of like Hostess Cupcakes. You know you're not supposed to eat them, but they're so good and somebody has to eat them or they'll just go to waste. Right? I poured my syrup over the pancakes and watched it slide down the sides, bringing a healthy dose of butter with it.

Then I heard familiar voices in the booth behind me. I gave Aunt Sissy a peculiar expression. I raised up on one knee, turned around, and found my husband and my stepfather looking over the menu in the next booth. "And just what in blazes are you doing here?" I asked with a smile on my face.

"Hey, honey," Rudy said.

I leaned over and tried to kiss him but couldn't quite reach his lips.

"We'll be over," he said. Since they hadn't ordered yet, they just got up and walked over to our booth. Rudy sat down next to me and gave me a kiss, while Colin just sort of looked at Aunt Sissy. He stood, his hands in his pockets, and looked around the room.

"Oh, all right," Aunt Sissy said and scooted over. Colin, reluctantly, sat down next to her.

"The lake get too lonely for you?" I asked.

"No, we got hungry," he said. "You think we just sit out on that boat all day without eating?"

"Not for a minute," I said. "I just thought you tore the heads off of the fish and sucked their guts out right then and there."

They each gave me a horrified expression.

"And no offense, but you stink."

"That's the down side to a fisherman."

"Yeah," I said.

"So, what are you guys up to?" Colin asked.

"Oh, nothing," I said with a downhearted tone.

Aunt Sissy stuffed a big forkful of blueberry pancakes into her mouth.

"No, seriously. What gives?" Colin asked. "You act like you lost your best friend. And that can't be possible, because I'm right here."

He actually had the nerve to smile. I think slapping one's stepfather should be perfectly acceptable behavior.

"Well, we found the girl," I said.

"The girl?" Colin asked.

"Oh, the one that wrote the book?" Rudy asked.

"Yeah. She died in a fire at, like, seventeen years of age. With a two-month-old baby to boot."

"Oh, how sad," Rudy said. "What was her name?"

"Anna Bloomquist."

"Bloomquist?" Colin asked.

"Yeah. Why?"

"That guy who rented us the fishing boat . . ." Colin said, snapping his fingers at Rudy. "His name was Bloomquist. Wasn't it? Billy or Bobby. Or, oh, what was it?"

"Brian," Rudy said.

"That's it. Brian," Colin said. "He owns a boat rental over on the other side of the lake. Wonder if he's related."

"Could be," I said. "Like a descendant of Sven. Or maybe another Bloomquist family moved into the area."

"What's the name of the boat rental?" I asked.

"Well, the sign said OLIN MARINA, BRIAN BLOOMQUIST, OWNER."

"Huh."

"What?" Rudy asked.

"I was just wondering why Roberta didn't mention that. How long has she lived here, Aunt Sissy?"

"Her whole life," she said with a mouthful of pancake.

"When I mentioned the Bloomquist name, she never said a word. She pointed out that the Hujinaks were still around, but never mentioned Brian," I said. "I just find that odd."

Nobody said anything for a minute. I waited for Aunt Sissy to swallow.

"Aunt Sissy, do you know Brian Bloomquist?"

She shrugged. "I see him from time to time, but don't really know him."

"What have you heard about him?"

"Not a lot of good. Sort of a rough fellow. Kids run around half naked and without shoes," she said.

"Huh."

"Huh what?" Colin asked. "Why do you keep saying huh?"

"It's just weird."

"Doesn't matter now, anyway," Aunt Sissy said. "We found out what we needed to find out."

"Well, but don't you think that somebody in the Bloomquist family would like to have the diary?" I asked.

"Wouldn't give Brian anything like that. He wouldn't take care of it."

"Is he the only one in the family? Does he have a sister? A brother?"

She shrugged again.

"Aunt Sissy, are you planning on keeping that manuscript? I mean, the diary?"

"It's a diary?" Rudy asked. "Oh, man."

"You should probably give it to the historical society if you're not going to give it to the family," I said.

"I haven't decided what I'm going to do with it," she said. "None of your business, anyway. I asked you to find out who wrote it and you did."

"Okay," I said. "All right. Calm down."

"I'm perfectly calm," she said and took another bite. "You better hurry up or I'm going to be finished eating. You haven't even started."

Colin gave me a puzzled look and picked up his menu. I took a bite of my pancakes. The waitress came and took the guys' orders. I couldn't take it anymore.

"I thought you wanted me to find out who wrote it so you

could give the manuscript to the rightful owner," I said.

"I never said that," Aunt Sissy said.

"But—"

"I never said that."

"You can't keep it."

"I most assuredly can keep it. In fact, I most probably will keep it."

"But—"

"You just hush up, Victory O'Shea. Do you hear me? I can keep it if I want," she said. I noticed the lines around her eyes and mouth had deepened just in the past few days. I couldn't help but wonder why I hadn't noticed that before. Her hands shook a little as she took a drink of her milk.

"Aunt Sissy, are you all right?"

"I'm fine. Don't much matter, anyway."

"What doesn't matter?" I asked.

Colin stood up. "I'm going to the rest room," he said. He gave Rudy a nod. I knew what the nod meant. It meant, Let's get out of here because this is going to get nasty.

Rudy followed suit with a look on his face that said he was glad to do it.

"What doesn't matter?" I asked again.

"It doesn't matter if I keep it. It's just going to be going to one of my kids shortly, anyway."

"Will you stop with the old remarks?" I said. "Jeez, you're not even seventy yet."

"It's my ticker," she said and pointed to her chest.

"What's your t—?" I stopped. "Aunt Sissy, what are you saying?"

"I'm saying that my ticker's going out on me. The doctor said I had a couple of years," she said.

"A couple of years? What are you talking about?"

"I'm dying, Torie. The only hope is a transplant and I'm not going to do that."

I was speechless. I couldn't do anything but sit there and stare at her. My stomach lurched and cramped and I felt like I was going to throw up all my pancakes right there and then. "Why?"

"Because I'm too old for a transplant. Good Lord, if they give me a new heart, I've got what? Ten years after that? No. I'm going to let somebody a little younger than me take the heart. That's it. It's over. I've got a couple of years and that's that."

I shook my head. "I just . . . I don't believe this."

"Believe it," she said. "Now finish your lunch."

"Finish my lunch!" I cried with tears burning the back of my eyes. "Are you insane? Finish my lunch?"

"I've come to terms with this, and if I can, you certainly can. So get over it."

Uncle Joe's words echoed through my head. "You haven't told anybody, have you?"

"You're the first."

"But—"

"They're all gonna act like you're acting right now. I don't want that. I figure I'll just drop dead and then they'll know," she said.

I swiped at a tear. What was wrong with my father's family? Why couldn't any of them face emotional confrontations like normal people? No, every one of them ran in the opposite direction just as fast as they could if it looked like things were going to get the least bit emotional. No wonder my mother had divorced my father.

"Oh, jeez," I said.

"You know what?" she said. "Fine. You can have the manuscript."

"No," I said. "I don't want it."

"Well, it's gotta go to somebody in a few years. Why don't you just take it now and save me the trouble later," she said.

"Because I don't want it."

"You're going to turn down your inheritance?" she asked. "What kind of niece turns down an inheritance?"

"If I take it, I'm just going to give it to the Bloomquists."

"You can do what you want with it. It's yours," she said.

"Aunt Sissy—"

"No, I'm serious."

Felicity "Sissy" Annabelle Keith Morgan was always serious, and especially when she said she was serious. You didn't dare cross her then.

"Don't be angry," I said.

"I'm not angry. I'm just . . . tired," she said and put another bite of pancakes in her mouth. "Now finish that food."

"Yes, ma'am," I said. I swallowed and fought back tears until I couldn't take it anymore. When I saw Colin and Rudy coming back to the table, I jumped up and ran to the ladies' room. I passed Rudy and gave him one of those silent married signals. The one that said "Don't bother me now, I'll tell you about it later." He let me go and I ran into the bathroom and cried in the sink.

Nine

"You mean she just told you right there behind her stack of blueberry pancakes that she was dying of heart disease?" Rudy asked.

He had stripped down to his boxers and stood at the foot of the bed staring at me. It was weird seeing my husband in nothing more than his boxers in somebody else's house. His cheeks were sunburned or windburned, I wasn't sure which, from being out on the boat two days in a row. It gave him a rather youthful appearance.

"Yes," I said. "I just can't believe it."

"And she hasn't told anybody else?"

"She said I was the first," I said, and flopped back on the stack of pillows. "I don't think she plans on telling any of them. I think she's just going to go about her business and when she dies, she dies."

"I've known your Aunt Sissy a long time," he said. "And if that's what she said, then that's what she intends to do. She is the only woman I've ever met who's more stubborn than you."

"Thanks," I said.

"Don't mention it," he said and crawled in bed next to me. He laid his head in the crook of my neck, wrapped his arm around me, and put one big hairy leg over my lower torso. I stared straight at the ceiling. Then I looked at the manuscript lying on the nightstand.

A few minutes went by as my attention flittered from one subject to the next. First it was the manuscript. I needed to finish reading it. But I wasn't sure I wanted to. Then it was the ceiling and I thought about how both houses that stood here before this one had succumbed to fire. And Roberta's words came back to me. How odd it was that this house and this property had never once been willed to anybody's heirs. It had always been sold to a stranger.

Rudy cleared his throat. "You gonna turn off the light?"

"No."

"No?" His voice seemed to come from somewhere small and distant.

"Do you believe in curses?"

"Yes," he said. "I married you, didn't I?"

I kicked him completely out of the bed. I heard a thud and then, "Oomph." A few seconds ticked by and then, "Jesus, woman. I think you broke my rib."

"Good. You deserved it."

"I was just joking," he said from the floor. He pulled himself up into the bed and did not come anywhere near me. "Okay, obviously my attempt at—"

"At what? Oh, please don't tell me that was foreplay. I've known you a long time. You can do way better than that."

He blushed. I love it when he blushes. "No, I was just teasing you. Trying to keep you from getting all somber on me."

"What? That makes no sense. I just told you my most favorite aunt in the world is dying and you're teasing me? How does that seem like a good idea to you?"

"Just . . . I just know you. You're thinking too much. Then you're going to start brooding and then before you know it, you'll be off half-cocked on some harebrained—"

"Just stop right there," I said.

"I was just trying to derail you," he said.

The phone rang and I jumped. It rang twice and somebody in the house picked it up. Within half a minute, Uncle Joe came to the door and said the phone was for me. I picked up the one next to the bed and said hello.

"Mom?"

"Rachel?" I said. I looked at the clock. Nine-forty. "Is everything all right?"

"Everything's fine," she said. "Gramma wanted me to call and let you know that Matthew's running a fever."

"Oh," I said.

"Don't worry, though. Collette's going to take him to the doctor tomorrow," she said. I had to smile. My best friend, Collette, stuck in a car with a toddler who was ill. But my mother, who was wheelchair-bound, couldn't exactly take Matthew to the doctor, so somebody had to do it. I thought it funny that my mother would think of Collette.

"All right," I said. "The insurance cards are in that envelope on the counter. Call me and let me know what the doctor says."

"I will," she said. She hung on the phone for a few seconds, just breathing. Rudy's eyebrows went up as if to ask if something was wrong. I gave him the everything's okay sign.

"Is there something else?" I asked.

"You have got to stop Mary."

"Now what?" Mary. My middle child. Three-fourths of the gray hairs in my head have her name on them. Since the day Mary was born nearly nine years ago, she has been the bane of her sister's existence. Rachel insists that life was perfect before Mary came along, and Mary insists that Rachel is a spoiled-rotten brat, sadly in need of a little sister to set her straight. This very thing has been going on since the dawn of time, right? I mean, somewhere back in prehistory, one sister hit the other sister over the head with a club because her sister ate her maggot. So you'd think in the eons of time since the invention of siblings that *somebody* would have found a cure for this.

"She called all of my friends and told them that I still sleep with my Pooh bear," Rachel said.

"Rachel. You do still sleep with your Pooh bear," I said. Yes, Rachel would be a teenager next year. Bras, boys, boy bands, but still there were stuffed bears.

"Yes, but that does not mean that she had to go off and tell everybody that! Now everybody at school is making fun of me," she said. I could hear the tears in her voice. Oh, the humiliation. The torture. This was a serious issue for a preteen in public school.

"So, just tell everybody that the Pooh bear was a gift from your long-dead grandmother and you promised her that you would sleep with it every night and that you just can't bear to break that promise to her."

"Mom. All of my grandmothers are still *living!*"

"Yes, but the kids at school don't know that. They only know about one of them."

"Aren't you going to do anything to your bratty daughter? This is so unfair. She goes off and does all these horrible, stinking things to me and you just laugh it off and make up lies for me to tell my friends. If she didn't do this stuff in the first place, you wouldn't have to think up these stupid stories, you know. It's so unfair. You always ignore what she does to me."

"I do not," I said.

At this point, Rudy had covered his head with a pillow.

"Put your sister on the phone," I said. A switch of hands and I heard something about how much trouble Mary was in and Mary saying something like *"Pthbbb!"*

"Hi, Mom," Mary said, bright and cheerful.

"Hi, Mary," I said. "Stop causing your sister so much grief."

"She is grief," Mary said.

"Stop it now, or I'll ground you."

"From what?"

"Does it matter?"

"Well, sure. If it's something I don't care about, then why should I stop?"

I swear to God, I just grew another gray hair. It went *bing*, right out the top of my head. "Whatever you ask me for in the next month, I will say no to. And before you agree to that, you think about it. A whole month. There will be something that you want really bad, or something that you ask me for, and I am going to say no, I don't care what it is."

"What if I ask if I can breathe? Or eat? Or pee?"

"Mary, for all that you hold dear, I swear . . ."

"Oh, all right," Mary said. "But she's such a baby."

"We've established that already. And I believe we've established that you're a brat. So, now let's be civil and move on. I love you."

"I love you, too," she said with all the gusto of a slug.

I heard her yell, "*Baby!*" at Rachel. Rachel got back on the phone. "She better straighten up, or I'm gonna kill her," Rachel said.

"You'll do no such thing," I said. "Be good. Your grandma doesn't need this. I'm going to bed. I love you."

"Love you, too. Bye."

I hung up the phone feeling completely exhausted. Rudy uncovered his head. "Well?"

"I took care of it."

"Lord," he said.

"It's a temporary condition. They become grown-ups one day," I said.

"I know," he said. "I was just wondering why we couldn't have had all boys."

I rolled my eyes and the manuscript on the nightstand caught my attention once again.

"Oh, go ahead and read it," he said. He picked up his pillow and took the top blanket off of the bed and headed for the door.

"Where are you going?"

"I'm going to go sleep with Colin," he said.

I tried not to laugh. "You might want to put something on other than boxers."

He looked down at himself. "Ugh," he said. He threw on his T-shirt and his sweatpants. "Good night."

"Thanks, honey. You're a sweetheart."

"No, I'm an idiot." He shut the door behind him and I

looked over at the manuscript. The diary. The detailed events of what had been a promising life. Did I really want to read it? Did I really want to know what led to her having a baby out of wedlock? Did I want to read about her heartache and pain when she realized that she and her lover would not be together? I thought about that. What had the little weasel said to her, I wondered? What could he possibly have said to her when she told him she was pregnant with his child? Whatever it was, it was bad. And what was the name of that weasel, anyway? For some reason, I wanted to know his name.

"Jeez," I said as I picked up the manuscript. "I'm pathetic."

About forty minutes later I had read about twenty-five pages. The handwriting got a little worse as it went, as if she were rushing to write it down. She wasn't taking her time or choosing her words quite so carefully. I suspected at this point that it was all about just getting it down. I tried to imagine that she was writing it for her daughter. I couldn't. Maybe she just wanted a record of it, so that one day her child would know exactly what her mother was feeling at that time. Maybe she didn't want Emelie to get the version that time had tempered.

I am desperate for word from my love. The last time we spoke, He told me that the parson had given Him strict instructions to stay away from me. The parson does not know who I am, but he knows that there is a special person in my lover's heart. I fear that if the parson finds out, he will tell my father before I have a chance to tell him myself. What sort of person would deny a man a wife? Deny him love?

Yes, what sort of person indeed? I found a pen on the night-stand but wasn't sure where my pad of paper was. It wasn't anywhere in the room, so I wrote on my hand: Parson's name?

Before I could pick the manuscript back up to continue reading, I heard a sound outside in the distance. I got up and walked to the window. It was dark, so I saw nothing. What did I expect?

I went back to reading:

> *The wolf bays lonesome tonight. I have not heard the two*
> *of them in nigh on a week. Just the one, just the female.*
> *Maybe the male has gone off to hunt. I wonder if they have*
> *cubs somewhere.*

There was the sound again. I went back to the window but couldn't see anything through the glare. What was it? I opened the door quietly and padded down the hallway to the steps. I opened the front door and stepped out onto the porch into the damp spring air and the sweet intoxicating smell of the lilacs. I'm not bothered by the cold too much, so the brisk temper-ature felt good on my face. I stood completely still, waiting for the sound.

And then I heard it.

No.

It couldn't be.

It sounded like a wolf.

Of course, would I know what the hell a wolf sounded like if I heard it? Maybe it was a coyote or a neighbor's dog. My skin felt like it rippled all the way down my arms. I remem-bered having this same feeling when I was in West Virginia and heard a panther in the middle of the night. But for some reason I wasn't afraid like I was when I heard the panther. Maybe it was because of all of those wildlife specials that talk about how there has never been a case of a wolf attacking a human. I don't know. Maybe I'm just stupid. Whatever the reason, I stepped off that porch and walked across the yard, behind the stables, and into the field.

As I went by the stables I startled one of the horses. "It's all right," I said. The horse didn't look as if it believed me, though. He trotted around the corral fence, uneasy with my presence this late at night. The field seemed smaller in the dark, but the thing I realized once I really looked around was that it wasn't *that* dark. There was a half moon tonight and the stars . . . How was it possible? When I looked up at the sky there were so many stars. This was the same sky we had in Missouri. Why did Minnesota have so many more stars? I suddenly felt small, and wholly insignificant.

And then I heard the rustle of leaves. "A wolf will not hurt me," I said. "It will not hurt me. *National Geographic* said it will not hurt me."

But what if it was a bear?

Just as I was ready to turn around and run, I saw something move on the edge of the forest. Then I spotted two golden eyes peering back at me through the cover of night and the thick foliage. I couldn't see the body that went with the eyes, but the eyes alone were enough to bewitch me. I was completely spellbound. My skin felt like it was shouting. I could feel every follicle on my head.

"What in the hell are you doing?"

I jumped and squealed and turned to find Colin standing

behind me. "Oh . . . you . . . man . . . God, don't ever do that to me," I said, placing my hand protectively over my heart. "Why aren't you sleeping?"

"Your husband snores."

I couldn't speak. I just stood there breathing in through my nose and out through my mouth, trying like heck to get my heart to calm down. My head was spinning from the sudden rush of blood.

"Are you going to answer me? Why are you out here? Are you trying to get eaten by a bear?" he asked.

"There are no bears here," I said. "No, I saw a wolf."

"A wolf."

"Yes, right there," I said and pointed to where the golden eyes had been just moments before.

"Okay, Torie, I was just joking about the bear thing," he said. "I'd be more concerned about a person being in those woods than a predator."

"No, I'm serious, Colin," I said. "I saw a wolf."

"Right."

"No, really."

"And just how many wolves have you seen in person?"

"I've seen a few at the Wolf Sanctuary back home."

"Torie . . ."

"No, really. I just saw a wolf," I said and then the realization hit me. "Oh, my God, I just saw a wolf."

"Yeah, whatever. Let's get inside before it eats us both. Besides, I'd be much more afraid of the ticks."

"Ticks?"

"Yes, the ticks here are horrible. I bet by the time we get back to the porch you've got two or three on your clothes."

"No," I said. I scratched the back of my head. Then behind my ear.

"Rudy and I were on the boat . . . on *water*, and I still found three ticks on me when I got in the shower. They're like commando ticks here."

Blood-sucking things are just disgusting. I scratched my collarbone.

I looked back at the woods and took a deep breath. I knew what I saw. I could feel the wolf in there looking back at me even now. Colin gestured toward the house with a jerk of his head. I followed him, reluctantly, across the field and back toward the house. We didn't speak to each other until we got to the porch.

"Don't tell anybody," I said.

"Tell anybody what?"

"That I saw a wolf."

He looked at me for a beat, as if trying to decide if I was insane or not. "Torie," he said. "I know that Minnesota has the largest wild wolf population in the country. But they don't come this far south. I saw it on *National Geographic*."

"You know for a fact that the wolves have never made it this far south?"

"I don't think they've ever been south of Duluth. And we are south of Duluth."

"All right," I said and held my hands up in surrender. But I knew better. I gave one quick glance toward the line of trees before I entered Aunt Sissy's house. It was a wolf. And it was still out there.

Ten

I was standing on the front porch of Aunt Sissy's house staring out at the lush green of the countryside around me when Rudy came outside holding a steaming mug of coffee in one hand and scratching his head with the other. He yawned, took a careful sip of the coffee, and then smiled. "Good morning."

"Good morning," I said.

"You're up early," he said.

True, it was still shy of six in the morning.

"I never went to bed."

"You . . . you what?" he asked.

"I never went to bed. I stayed up and read that blasted diary all night."

"Good thing I slept in Colin's room," he said.

"Yeah, you would have lost it when I started crying."

"You . . . you were crying?"

"It's just such a sad story, Rudy. And now that I know it was a *true* story and that it actually happened to somebody . . ."

91

I stared off, clipping my words in time to keep from crying all over again.

"What happened?" he asked.

"Oh, man, Rudy. I am so glad we live in this century."

"Okay . . . What happened?"

"Well, there are these long periods of time in the diary where she just describes the long days of hard work and her and her brother watching the rabbits play in the field . . . that sort of thing. But then, then there are passages between her and her lover that are just these blazing love scenes. I mean, I blush and skip entire paragraphs."

"Really?" he asked, a little too interested.

I shot him a look and he shrugged.

"I just didn't know . . . you know, that they had sex back then."

"Excuse me?" I asked.

"I mean, I know they had sex, but not, you know . . . the kind you enjoy."

"Oh," I said. "Well, it's safe to say that our forefathers knew a little bit more than we realize."

"And? What else happened?"

"Well, she got pregnant. That's what happened. The other side of the coin of pleasure is usually some sort of penance."

"Oh," he said.

"Anyway, in this diary, she talks about this evil, evil parson. I mean this man was just horrible. Evidently, her lover was the parson's apprentice or son or pupil of some sort. Maybe he was just his valet or helping hand. Whatever it was, the parson held some sort of sway over Anna's lover. I kept wondering why they just didn't court outright, in front of everybody. But it was all done in secret. The lover, he kept making statements like, 'Not here, or somebody will see.' I mean, why couldn't they just court and set a wedding date like normal people?" I said. "Maybe then, they wouldn't have felt the need to . . . have sex. Okay, that sounded stupid. But maybe if they knew they would for sure be together one day, they could have held off. They could have abstained. But I think they were so desperate to be together for the simple fact that they never knew if they were going to get to be together. Does that make sense?"

Rudy shrugged his shoulders. "Yeah, that makes sense. But it doesn't necessarily mean that they would have abstained."

"I know."

Rudy thought for a moment. "Maybe they couldn't get married because it was somehow forbidden by the boy's religion."

"But why? I mean, they were Lutherans. As far as I know, the Lutheran Church does not put restrictions on their clergyman getting married," I said. "If he were studying to be a priest . . . well, then *that* I could understand."

I was quiet a moment. Stifling a yawn, I looked at my husband and decided that he needed to be hugged. I gave him a good, long, firm hug. He kissed the top of my head and stroked my hair with his free hand.

"You're happy, right?" I asked.

"Happy with what?"

"Us. You know, our marriage. I know I can be a bit . . ."

He opened his mouth to say something and I stopped him.

"Just don't answer that," I said.

We were both quiet again. "So what else happened in the diary? Just the fact that she got pregnant shouldn't have been enough to make you cry," he asked.

"Well, I know this sounds strange, but there were these wolves in the diary. These two wild wolves that lived here on the property. And the wolves' story sort of parallels Anna's story," I said.

"How so?"

"The farmers found a few animals missing. You know, a bloody trail leading into the woods," I said. "A pig here, a sheep there . . ."

"Everywhere an oink-oink."

"Oh, you're too funny," I said.

"I'm sorry," Rudy said. "Go ahead."

"Think about it, Rudy. Here's an animal who is a predator. It hunts to survive. And sometimes the pickings are slim. Suddenly, man moves into its territory and what does man do? Man brings all these pigs, cows, and sheep and confines them. Man has brought the wolf dinner and put it in a box so it can't run away from the wolf. I mean, what wolf in its right mind is going to go after a wild deer that it might have to chase ten miles and then still might not catch, when it can just walk over to Farmer John's house and take one of those little pigs that are inside a fence and can't run away? Well . . . the farmers . . ."

"They killed the wolves," Rudy said.

"At first they just killed the male. They hunted him down, killed him, took his pelt as a souvenir," I said. "They left the female to mourn and try and take care of their young on her own."

"And?" Rudy asked.

I just stared at him.

"Well?" he asked. Then he realized what I wasn't saying. "Anna's lover?"

"According to Anna, the parson beat her lover to death and hung him in her father's barn."

"What?" Rudy's eyes grew wide. It was unfathomable. He couldn't digest it. I could see it in his eyes.

"Now, I don't know how Anna knew that it was the parson, or if she just suspected it was the parson," I said. "But either way, the lover ended up dead and hanging in her barn. It was awful."

"So then what happened?" he asked, and took another sip of his coffee. A bigger gulp this time, since it had had time to cool off.

"So, then Anna wanted to die. She spent days just lying around and refusing all nourishment. Her mother was frantic, but her father . . . her father felt as though she had deserved what she had gotten. He told her, if you sin, you will be punished."

"Pretty heartless," Rudy said.

"Well, he cried along with her. And she talks about how her father eventually came to her and told her that no matter what, he did love her," I said. "But it was Anna's brother, Sven, who really brought her around. He told her she had to eat or the baby would die, and then all that existed of her lover would be gone for good. So Anna began eating."

"And the baby was born," Rudy said.

"Yes, the baby was born. And her diary literally skips most of the pregnancy. Things were quiet for a while," I said.

"Until?"

"Until the farmers found the female wolf."

Rudy's expression darkened. "I don't want to know," he said. "Why do you get involved in this kind of thing?"

"Aunt Sissy is the one who asked me to read it," I said. "Knowing what I know, I couldn't *not* finish it."

"Okay, so what happened?" he asked.

"They trapped the she-wolf in a neighbor's shed. Some old building that the neighbor was going to tear down anyway. Then they burned it down. With the wolf inside."

Rudy just shook his head.

"Oh, but the worst part is Anna . . . She somehow knew what was coming. She said in her diary, 'I know I shall suffer the same fate as the she-wolf. Our destinies are intertwined. But at least her cubs survived. Maybe Emelie will live on.' Lord, Rudy. I just put those papers aside and bawled like a baby."

"Because Emelie dies with her mother in the fire."

"Yes," I said. "Two months old. It's more than I could think about. Anna knew when she was trapped in that cellar that her baby was going to die with her."

I swiped at a tear.

Rudy hugged me close. "See, this is why I'm happy," he said.

"What?" I asked. "What are you talking about?"

"I'm happy because I'm married to a woman who cries over a baby and a wolf and a girl whom she never knew, and who lived a hundred and fifty years ago," he said.

"Oh, jeez," I said and sniffled. I pulled a tissue out of my pocket and swiped at my nose.

"So, what's the last entry in the diary?" Rudy asked.

"Emelie's baptism. Anna took her to Cedar Springs to have her baptized. She wouldn't have her baptized here in Olin, at her church. She said that even though the parson was now gone, she couldn't bear to have Emelie baptized there. I guess the parson moved on," I said. "According to Anna, it was a gorgeous day. She went only with her brother. Her parents wouldn't go. And she cried at the thought of her lover looking down from heaven upon his little girl's dedication to God."

"Man," Rudy said. "What an amazing story."

"I know now why Aunt Sissy didn't want to part with the manuscript. I don't want to part with it either, because I want to make sure that whoever has it will really appreciate it. I can't stand the thought of somebody tossing it in a wet basement or using it for kindling, or letting their kids color on the backs of the pages. But, yet . . . I don't want to keep it either."

"So, what are you going to do with it?"

"Well, I think I'm going to come along fishing with you guys and see if Mister Bloomquist is the descendant of Sven. Of course, he probably won't know if he is descended from Sven. But if he is, then I'm going to check him out first. If he seems ruthless and heartless, you know, like somebody who could care less about a manuscript written by his great-great-grandfather's sister, then I'm going to donate it to the historical society. At least there I know it will be taken care of. Maybe I'll stop in the cities and see if there is a depository of some sort for historical manuscripts. In Minneapolis or St. Paul, it will most likely be read and at least preserved. I feel like Anna deserves that," I said.

"You know," Rudy said, "there are millions of stories like Anna's down through the ages. She wasn't the only one."

"I know, but she's the only one who told me her story in her voice."

"I understand," Rudy said. He took a big deep breath and sighed. "I think I smell breakfast. And I think I hear the fish calling my name."

"Yeah," I said. "Hey, you and Colin won't care if I tag along today, right?"

"No, I don't care," Rudy said.

I turned around to find Colin standing in the doorway. "So, you're fishing with us today?" he asked.

"Looks like it."

"Hope you can swim. Because I'm terrible about tipping the boat over."

"Ha, ha, ha," I said.

Colin smiled, but there was something in his eyes that wasn't humor.

"What's the matter?" I asked. He said nothing. "Were you listening to our conversation?"

He blushed and shrugged his shoulders. "I was coming to get Rudy for breakfast . . . I couldn't help but hear it."

"How long did you stand there? You could have said something," I said.

"I wanted to hear how the story ended," he said. But his eyes were communicating more than that. He had been there last night. When I saw the wolf. I wondered at that moment if he had actually seen the wolf, too.

"I'm starving," I said.

"Oh, your aunt made pork chops for breakfast," he said. "The woman is my hero."

"If I had known that all it would take was breakfast chops to make you respect me, I would have made them for you a long time ago," I said.

"Yeah, but you can't cook," Colin said.

"I can so! Rudy, you had better come to my defense or you will be sorry," I said.

"She makes wonderful cereal," Rudy said. "The best in two counties."

Eleven

Olin Lake was beautiful in the morning light. The sunlight looked like little golden flakes of glitter floating on top of the water. The Olin Marina was a nice establishment, with scores and scores of boats docked out in front of it. Off to the left was a sign advertising the rental boats. Probably another ten or so boats, all uniform in design, were resting there. Rudy pulled the truck into the parking lot and we got out and walked into the marina.

"So these boats over here, do they belong to the locals?" I asked Rudy.

"As far as I can tell, all of those boats belong to people who don't have lakefront property and want to keep their boats in the water."

"How big is this lake?" I asked as I shielded my eyes from the sun and looked out across water that had no end.

"It's about twice as big as White Bear Lake," Colin said.

"And how big is that?"

"I don't know," Colin said. "Big."

The marina had a restaurant and rest rooms inside, along with a bait shop that sported rods and reels, battery-operated socks, you name it. You could even get your fishing license here. The man behind the counter was just a kid, really. He was maybe eighteen or nineteen. He smiled as soon as he saw Rudy and Colin. "Hello, gentlemen," he said. "Your boat's waiting for you."

I looked at Rudy.

"We rented a boat for the whole week."

"I thought you guys were going to try out a few of the lakes."

"We liked this one so much, we decided not to mess with it," Colin said.

"Oh," I said.

"This is my wife, Torie," Rudy said. "She's coming out with us today."

The kid nodded and waved.

"Um, I was wondering . . . Are you a Bloomquist? Are you the owner?" I asked.

"No," he said. "I just work here. Saving up for college."

"I see," I said. "Is Mr. Bloomquist in?"

"Brian? No, he won't be in until about noon," he said.

"Thank you," I said. I turned to Rudy. "You guys can bring me back around noon, can't you? I mean, you stop for lunch anyway, right?"

"Sure," he said. "Not a problem."

And so we headed out onto the lake. I have to admit, I was a little excited as the boat zoomed away from the marina. Even if I didn't like to fish, I still loved being out on the water. I had brought my camera along and began snapping pictures almost as soon as my butt was in the boat. Colin made me put a life jacket on. At first I couldn't figure out what good that would do my camera if we capsized, but then I realized he was concerned for my well-being. Golly, gee. Twice in one vacation.

It wasn't long until Colin had a nibble, and then almost before I could get the camera aimed, he brought the fish up out of the water and I snapped the picture. An hour or so went by and I was just enjoying the lap of the water against the boat, smelling the water . . . and okay, the fish smell was a little irritating, but I tried not to let it bother me. Rudy finally caught a fish, and I got to snap a picture of him, too. Then I asked Colin to take one of me and Rudy. He took three or four.

"Hey, you should get your picture made with Colin," Rudy said. "I don't think there's a picture of the two of you since his wedding."

"So?"

"Come on," Rudy said. "Get over there."

"Oh, all right," I said. I scooted over by Colin and put my arm around him. "Hi, Dad."

Rudy snapped the picture just as Colin rolled his eyes. "I can't believe you share the same genetic material as my wife," Colin said.

"Oh, I don't pretend one bit that my mother didn't get all the good genes, because she did. My mother's perfect," I said.

"Well, as perfect as a woman can be," he said. At first I thought he was serious and I had my fist all balled up and was ready to just knock him into the water when he started cracking up laughing. "Sorry. I tried to keep a straight face."

Things went back to being quiet. I kept looking through

my camera lens trying to find just the right picture of the lake. I snapped a few pictures and then we were ready to head in for lunch break. As we approached the marina, I couldn't help but notice how quaint it looked. It would have been a classic piece of Americana if it weren't for the falling-down boat shack on the property next to it.

We got out of the boat and I stretched and screamed. "Oh my God, I have a crick in my back. Oh, jeez, oh, jeez, oh, jeez." Rudy rubbed the middle of my back with the palm of his hand, while Colin just rolled his eyes and waited patiently. "I'm sorry, I'm not used to sitting in one position all day."

I hobbled into the marina to find a different man standing behind the counter. I tried to remember how Aunt Sissy and Roberta had described Brian Bloomquist. He didn't seem all that bad. I walked up to the counter and smiled. "Mr. Bloom-quist?"

"Yes," he said. "I'm Brian."

He was about forty or forty-five, really tall and really blond, with dark, smoky eyes. "Hi," I said. "I'm Torie O'Shea, and I'm here from St. Louis, visiting my aunt." Since St. Louis is the closest city of any size to my hometown of New Kassel, I always just tell people that I'm from St. Louis when I'm on vacation. It's too hard to explain exactly where New Kassel is.

"Glad to have you," he said.

"Yes, and I was wondering if I could ask you a few questions?"

"What sort of questions?" he asked. "You can tell Kimberly Canton my answer is still no."

"Uh . . . this has nothing to do with that, whatever that is. This is a more personal matter," I said.

"What did she do now?"

"Who?"

"My ex-wife," he said.

"No, it's not that personal," I said.

"Well, then, what the hell do you want?" he asked. He was obviously confused, and the lines between his eyebrows sort of gave that away.

"I was wondering how much of your family tree you know?"

"What, like my great-great-grandpa and all that crap?"

"Yes," I said. Okay, maybe he wasn't the best candidate for ownership of a hundred-and-fifty-year-old diary. "On the Bloomquist side. I was trying to track down somebody in a particular branch of the family."

"Is there money involved? If so, I'm descended from whoever I have to be," he said and smiled.

"No," I said.

The expression on his face fell from the pure elation just moments ago when he thought he might actually have money coming. "Oh, uh . . . I know that my grandpa's dad, my great-grandpa, he was mayor of Olin back in, like, the turn of the century," he said.

"Which century?"

"Oh, you know like 1902 or somewhere around there."

"Do you know his name?"

"Mmmm, boy, let me think," he said. He looked at the ceiling for a few seconds. "Seems to me I wanna say John."

"Is that as far back as you know?" I asked.

"Yeah," he said.

"Any other tidbits of info? Any family legends that you know of? Anything you can give me will help," I said. "I'm trying to figure out if it's the same Bloomquists. Like, do you know where your family came from originally? Where they lived?"

"Mmm, Dad told me once that the Bloomquists were from Sweden, and that they'd lived here for a long time. Well, my dad grew up in town, but I think somewhere back there somebody owned a farm—but like that's a real help. Most people before 1900 owned a farm, right?"

"Right," I said.

Brian looked around the room, his gaze landing on a few customers. I knew that he was getting antsy and wanted to take care of business.

"Well, thank you, Mr. Bloomquist," I said.

"Oh, call me Brian."

"Brian."

"Did I help any?"

"Yes," I said, although I wasn't sure how much. "Still haven't made the connection yet, but if I do, I'll let you know."

"Great," he said. "In the meantime, enjoy the lake."

I caught up with Rudy and Colin at the front door. "Well, did he know who Anna was?" Rudy asked.

"Nah," I said. "I just asked how far back he could go on his family tree and he remembered that his great grandpa was once the mayor of Olin. John was his name. That's probably one or two generations removed from Sven, still."

"Oh, that's too bad," Rudy said.

"So, what are you going to do with the manuscript?" Colin asked.

"Well, I think I'm going to check out John. If he was mayor, there has to be some information on him somewhere. I want to find out who his parents and grandparents were. If he is descended from Sven, then I want to try and find other descendants, other than just Brian."

"Why?" Colin asked. "Can't you just give the manuscript to Brian?"

"I think what Torie is trying to say," Rudy said, "is she wants to find somebody more appreciative."

"Exactly," I said. "Brian was really only interested in what I had to say because he thought I was going to have long-lost money for him."

"Oh," Colin said. "Well, what if you don't find anybody who is appreciative enough?"

"I don't want to think about that," I said. "I'm also going to check out the Evil Parson."

"Huh?" Rudy asked.

"You know, the bad guy from the diary. It sucks, hating some anonymous jerk. I want him to have a name. So, I'm going to find him one," I said.

We all walked out to the truck, my stomach rumbling all the way. I was as hungry as Colin lately. The tumbledown shack on the land next to the marina caught my attention again. "Hey, how much do you think lakefront property is worth up here?"

"Oh, a lot," Colin said. "Why?"

"I just can't figure out why somebody would let a piece of property like that go," I said. "I mean, if you can't afford to keep the building painted, why not just sell it?"

"Who knows?" Rudy said. "Does it bother you that much?"

"Well, it's such an eyesore. I mean, look at all the rest of the lakefront. It's beautiful. It figures, there has to be a bad apple in every bunch," I said.

"So, where're we eating?" Colin asked.

"Pancake Palace," Rudy said.

Twelve

Instead of going back out on the lake with Rudy and Colin, I decided to look around the town a bit. I agreed to be back at the marina at five to pick them up from their day of fishing. I drove to the city limits and parked the truck and walked through town. In the center of Olin was a public notice board with messages posted on it. They were mostly things like fliers announcing that bingo night had changed, a pet had been lost, a baby-sitter was needed. A bright orange and black flier advertised the strongman competition this weekend. And there were a few other more official-looking notices about an estate, and an auction. Then, right there in the middle was one that just leapt out at me. It was an announcement of a monument that was to be erected during the festival this week in honor of the founder of the city of Olin.

I walked over to the historical society and hoped that Roberta would be there. Out front was sitting the same little red

Geo Metro that had been there yesterday, so I knocked on the door and entered.

As I barreled through the door, I saw Roberta suddenly jump. "Oh, sorry. I didn't mean to startle you," I said.

Roberta looked past me and I glanced over my shoulder. An attractive woman stood behind me, inspecting a photograph that hung on the wall. She turned and smiled at me. She was breathtaking to look at. Very fresh-faced and earthy, and yet exotic at the same time. "Oh, hello."

The woman smiled at me and said something about it being a nice day, to which I couldn't do anything but nod and agree with her. Roberta came over to me then. "What can I do for you?"

"I just saw a public notice about a monument being erected for the founder of the city," I said.

"Yes?"

"Well, it made me think to ask you about him and ask you . . ." I glanced over at the woman. ". . . about a lot of things. Would you happen to have a book of biographical sketches?"

She looked confused. Maybe she just didn't know which of my questions to answer first, but I explained what I was looking for.

"It's a book that is usually made up of biographical sketches of important leaders of the community: political, parochial, educational. I mean, you may not have one just for Olin, but you might have one for the whole county," I said.

"Of course," Roberta said. "Yes, I know exactly what you're talking about." She walked over and pulled two books off of the shelf behind her desk. They were ancient. The one was at least a century old, the other about eighty years old.

"Oh, please tell me they're indexed," I said. I get so irritated with these old books, because they are rarely ever indexed and you have to look at every page to find what you need.

"Well, the older one isn't indexed, but it is in alphabetical order. I'm afraid the other one is not indexed, nor is it in alphabetical order. I'm not sure how they put the book together. Somebody told me once that they thought it was geographical. That the author just started at one end of the county and went to the next. Pretty strange way to put a book together."

"Boy, I'll say," I said. I glanced over at the guest once again. "Can I just stand here and look through these?"

"Certainly," Roberta said.

I tackled the alphabetical one first. I'd have been an idiot to do otherwise. In the meantime, Roberta sat back down at her desk. The problem was that this book was written far too early to have anything about John Bloomquist, since he didn't become mayor until around 1900. Of course, one thing I've learned since becoming a genealogist is that rarely do people ever get dates or names correct when talking about their ancestors. Unless they are genealogists, too. So, I checked anyway.

There was something on Sven. I couldn't believe it.

"Roberta, do you have a copier here?"

"No, 'fraid not. You'd have to go over to the post office."

"The post office–grocery store?"

"Right."

"Can I take this book over there?"

She shrugged. "I'm really not supposed to let you," she said.

"I can give you paper and pen and you can copy it down."

"Yes, but there's a photograph in here I'd like to get a copy of."

"Oh . . ."

"Please? I swear to you I will bring it right back."

"All right," she said. "But only because I know your aunt will deliver you to me if you go back on your word."

"Thank you," I said. I tried to remember some of the other names that I had looked up in the land records. I couldn't remember the dates that any of them had owned the house that my aunt now lived in. But I knew the Hujinaks didn't come along until later. Hendrickson. That one I could remember. I looked it up and there wasn't a chapter on that last name.

"Roberta, do you remember the list of people who owned my aunt's farm before her? I just can't remember everybody's name."

"Um, the Olsons, the Hujinaks . . . Reed. Wendell Reed."

"That's right, but I don't think he moved in until after 1900 sometime. Then came the Hendricksons. And then there was one other between them and the Bloomquists."

Roberta cleared her throat and appeared a little antsy. "I believe it was Rogers."

"That's right. So blasted simple, of course I forgot it."

Just as I was about to check the book for the Rogers name, the woman who had been observing the photographs on the wall thanked Roberta for her help, told her to have a nice day, and left.

"James Rogers," I said to myself, and turned the pages to the R's. "James Rogers, wealthy banker from Philadelphia, moved his family to Minnesota just at the outbreak of the Civil

War. He bought a lumber company and prepared to make a fortune here on the frontier. His oldest son went off to war and died at Gettysburg. After that, Mrs. Rogers, a God-fearing and good woman, began a coalition for grieving parents of Union Veterans. James, whose family was English in origin, started his business along the St. Croix River. He bought the old farm and house on the old Pine Road, where tragedy had befallen the Swedish family of Bloomquists just a few years before. He rebuilt the house and settled his family in for the long haul."

I stopped and worked my lip between my fingers.

"What's wrong?" Roberta asked.

Her voice startled me, because I had totally forgotten that I was standing in her office or that I was reading out loud. "Nothing, it's just that Aunt Sissy said the house was rebuilt in 1878, which would have been when the Hendricksons owned it."

"So?"

"Well, James Rogers had to have either rebuilt the house or made major repairs to it or something, or his large family couldn't have lived there for nearly seventeen years."

"So?"

"It's nothing," I said. "It's just that any time there's a discrepency in the story, it sort of calls out to me. Aunt Sissy's real estate agent or whoever it was who told her the history of the house could have easily gotten things confused."

I went back to reading. Rogers Logging became a successful company, and then one day he sold his company and moved out West. I turned the pages. "They have a picture of the house!" I said.

"What?" she asked.

"They have a picture of the house he lived in. Oh, that is too cool."

"What are you looking for now?" Roberta asked. "Sissy told me you two found out who the girl was."

"Yeah," I said. "We did. But now I'm trying to find out more about the family and a little about the area that she lived in. Help me fill in the blanks more. And I want to see if I can find a member of her family who would like to have the manuscript."

"Oh," she said, her eyes growing wide. "You could donate it here, to the historical society. We'd love to have it."

"I know," I said. "Believe me, I'm considering it. I just want to make an offer to the family first. If they're not interested, then it will probably go to you."

She smiled from ear to ear. "What else can I do to help?"

"Have you read the novel, the diary, that my aunt has?"

"No," she said.

"Well, I was really hoping to find out who the parson or preacher was at the Lutheran church in about 1858. Is there a shortcut to find that out?"

She laughed and then covered her mouth with the back of her hand. "I'm sorry. I shouldn't laugh, you're not from around here."

"No," I said. "What's so funny?"

"Well, there's no shortcut needed," she said.

"Why not?"

"Well, because most everybody knows who that was. The kids are taught that in school, when they're taught local history," she said.

I was confused. "Why? I mean, why would that one person

be plucked out of the past to be taught to the school kids?"

"Because Nagel's the founder of Olin. The one you were asking about. He's a hero around here."

"A hero."

"Yes," she said. "And my ancestor. One of the reasons he's actually getting a monument is because his great-great-great-granddaughter is the president of the historical society. Me."

I was too stunned to speak.

"He was a German immigrant to Lancaster County, Pennsylvania. You know, those Pennsylvania Dutch," she said.

"Yes," I said, trying to act as if I hadn't just had the socks shocked off of me. "My husband has an ancestor who actually founded Germantown. I'm familiar with the Pennsylvania Dutch. But I thought they were usually Mennonites or Amish or Quakers. My husband's were Mennonites."

"Well, sure. But evidently Konrad Nagel decided that wasn't the religion for him. He headed West, founded Olin, and started the Olin Lutheran Church," she said.

My head hurt. I sort of listened to her titter on about Mr. Nagel, the hero, without really paying attention. This couldn't be right. They were going to erect a monument to the man who had murdered Anna's lover?

"Wait," I said. "You're sure he was the preacher during the year 1858?"

"He was the head of the church, right over there on Sixth Street, from 1854 until 1861, when he was murdered."

"Murdered. Did you say murdered? You have an ancestor who was murdered?"

"Oh, yes. Terrible thing it was. Some stranger came to town during a blizzard and needed a place to stay. Konrad opened his doors to him and told him he could stay as long as he needed. The man killed him in the middle of the night."

"You're sure? How can you be sure?"

"Everybody knows that story. I mean, it's known for three counties. The founder of a city, and a man of the cloth, can't be butchered in the middle of the night by some stranger—whom he opened his doors to—and it not become known. *That* is the stuff of legends, for Pete's sake. Besides, my grandma used to tell me stories about it. When it's in the family, it sort of gets handed down."

"Of course," I said. I swiped at my brow and ran my fingers through my hair. I knew the book I held would have a nice big biography on Mr. Nagel. And it would most likely have a picture of him. I wasn't so sure I wanted to look at his face. But, at the same time, what if the bio mentioned his apprentice?

Roberta went on. "Especially since his son had been brutally murdered as well. Two murders in a county with a population of maybe twelve hundred people, in the mid-nineteenth century . . . Well, that's not only what legends are made of, but it's headlines, too. I think the story was printed all the way down in the cities."

His son. He had killed his own son? "So . . . he became a martyr, that son-of-a—"

"Mrs. O'Shea?" Roberta asked. "What's wrong?"

"Nothing," I said. "So, obviously, Mr. Nagel had to have had more than one child. Right? Or are you descended from the son who was murdered?"

"No," she said. I sighed with relief. "I'm descended from his daughter, Isabelle. She was already married and had moved out by the time Konrad moved here with Isaac."

"Isaac?"

"His son. The one who was murdered."

Oh, Lord. The lover's name was Isaac. I had discovered the lover's name!

"For some reason there are eleven years between Isabelle and Isaac," she said. "Isabelle lived over in Cedar Springs. My grandma moved here, to Olin, in the 1920s. I was born here," she said.

I just nodded my head. What could I say?

"So, why were you so interested in who the parson was over at the Lutheran church? Does Anna Bloomquist mention him in her diary?" she asked, her eyes full of stars. I knew what that was all about. I can't tell you how many times I've fantasized that somebody, somewhere, had left a written record of a particular ancestor and how I would just happen to stumble upon it one day. Unfortunately, most of the time on the frontier, the people left nothing as personal as a diary or letters or a history. I found it a miracle if one could actually find a Bible record. Back East was a different story. Out on the frontier, the prairie, they were just too worried about surviving.

The seconds seemed to stretch out to minutes as I tried to think of what to say to her. I didn't want to lie to her. But obviously she wasn't prepared for the truth. Neither was the town, for that matter. And I couldn't give her the diary. Not now. Once she read it she would know who it was. Especially since I'd been inquiring about him.

"Uh . . ."

"Well?" she asked.

"I'm not sure. I'll have to read more of it."

"Maybe I could read it," she said. "I would recognize him if she wrote about him."

"Oh. No. That's . . . okay. I'm going to go make copies of

these real quickly. All right? I'll be right back," I said and got the heck out of there. Holy cow, how do I get myself into these predicaments?

The grocery store was on the opposite side of town. I had to pass the Lutheran church as I walked over to make the copies. I just stared at the church as I walked by. I wanted to go inside. I wanted to walk to the cemetery. But first I had to make copies.

The grocery store was an old white brick building, with a silver metal awning that hung out over the sidewalk. There were decals on the windows advertising all the credit cards that they took, bread that was forty-nine cents a loaf, and Zest that was buy one, get one free. I went to the counter and asked where the copy machine was and the woman pointed me toward the back of the store, where the post office was. I made my copies, staring into the room with the postal clerk and the little rows of brass mail boxes. I wondered if this was one of those towns where the residents had a rural route address, plus a box at the post office. New Kassel used to be like that until about ten years ago, and now we just get our mail delivered to the house. Before that, everybody had to go to the post office to get their mail.

I had to have one of the cashiers make change for my five-dollar bill, because the copier only took dimes and nickels. When I finished, I turned to leave and found Roberta standing behind me with her hands on her hips.

"Hi, Roberta. I was just on my way back with the books," I said.

She put one hand out, palm up. I put the books in her hand. Honest, I wasn't going to keep them.

"Is there a problem?"

She stepped up close to me. "I don't know who you think you are, or what you think you're up to. But I remembered Sissy telling us all at a prayer meeting one time that the novel she was reading—the one you both determined to be a diary— had a minister in it who was mean and abusive."

I hung my head. What could I say?

"And now you're suddenly all interested in Konrad Nagel. I'm not stupid. I may not come from a *fancy* historical society, where I get to wear big poofy dresses and give tours in big gigantic houses, but I can put two and two together. And if you think for one minute—no, make that one second—that my ancestor is the man Anna wrote about in her diary . . . you are *so, so, so, so, so* mistaken."

People were gathered now, looking over the rack of Hostess Cupcakes and from behind the display of Doritos.

"I . . . Roberta . . ."

"That's Mrs. Flagg, to you," she said.

"I don't know what to say. The evidence is there," I said.

"Don't you evidence me!"

"But—"

"How would you feel if it were your ancestor?"

"Well, actually, I had a similar thing happen in my family," I said. "We are who we are, Roberta. I mean, Mrs. Flagg. What came before us is before us. You have no bearing on Konrad Nagel's behavior. You can't be held responsible for his actions. I mean, you wouldn't be who you are if you weren't descended from him. A good him or a bad him. You're still you because of him. So, you just have to accept it."

She just stood there with her mouth open, staring at me as if I had just said the most preposterous thing ever uttered on the earth.

But I understood this reaction. Just as some people think they are better than everybody else because they're descended from some Revolutionary War hero, or the king of England, so it must mean that they are somehow worse than everybody else if they are descended from horse thieves, indentured servants, and ax murderers. Which is silly, of course. Especially if you didn't even know those people were your ancestors to begin with. So how can your status be elevated or lowered once you find it out? It was really silly, but a common reaction nonetheless.

"Look, Mrs. O'Shea, the only thing I've ever had going for me in this godforsaken existence that I call my life is that I have a great pedigree! I've got nothing else. I've got a two-timing husband, children who don't respect me, a nonexistent career, and a mother who despises the ground I walk on. You will not take Konrad Nagel from me. Do I make myself clear?" she said.

"Yes," I said. "Perfectly."

"Now, you just take yourself right on back to your aunt's house and stay there until it's time for you to go back to your fancy little historical society," she said. "We don't need outsiders meddling in our affairs and rewriting history."

"Even if it needs rewriting?" I asked.

The next thing I knew her fist had slammed square in my eye and I was looking at the water-stained ceiling from flat on my back.

Thirteen

I can't believe that bitch hit you!" Aunt Sissy said. She handed me a steak. "Here, put this on your eye."

"I will not!" I said. "That's gross. You put a dead carcass on *your* eye. Get me some ice."

"Well, aren't we in a bad mood," Aunt Sissy said. She proceeded to get me some ice out of her freezer and place it in a Ziploc bag.

"I just got punched in the eye and now you're trying to put a dead cow on my face. Why wouldn't I be in a bad mood?" I laid the ice next to my eye and nearly screamed, it hurt so bad.

Uncle Joe came into the kitchen about that time, walked over to the gun case, and got out his shotgun. He came back into the kitchen and loaded it. "Uncle Joe, she just hit me, that's all."

"Who hit you?" he said. When he looked up he did a double take. "What the hell happened to your eye?"

"Roberta Flagg punched her," Aunt Sissy said. "Can you believe it? That woman sure takes her genealogy seriously."

I sighed with relief. The gun was not for Roberta. "Uncle Joe, why are you getting out your twelve-gauge?"

"Found another . . . well, what's left of another animal," he said.

"So you're going to shoot it?" I asked.

"No, we think it might be a wolf that's killing the livestock."

"A wolf!" I screeched. "No!"

Uncle Joe and Aunt Sissy gave me pretty much identical stares of disbelief. Like I had lost my mind, along with my eyesight and the teeny-weeny trace of beauty I'd had to begin with. "It can't be a wolf."

"Why not?" Uncle Joe asked.

"Th-they don't come this far south. *National Geographic* said so."

Uncle Joe waved a hand at me. "Torie, I don't think *National Geographic* has ever done a special on Minnesota gray wolves," he said. "But I can tell you, the wolves have been moving farther and farther south lately. They're getting much bolder."

"Well, what do you expect?" I asked before I could stop myself. "I mean, you're dangling their food source out in front of them and then getting mad when they eat it. How are they supposed to know the difference? They're just dumb animals, right?"

"Well, then, if it's so dumb, it won't mind when I put this barrel between its eyes and pull the trigger, now will it?"

I gasped. "Uncle Joseph!"

"You just keep your nose out of stuff," he said. "Before somebody punches it, too."

"Okay, that's it," I said. "I'm leaving."

"You will do no such thing," Aunt Sissy said.

"The hell I won't," I said. "You people are crazy. You asked me up here to read . . . to read this, this *morbid* diary about a girl who dies in a fire and a minister who's the founder of the city who killed his own son and people who kill animals for just being who they are. You just remember something, Uncle Joe. *We* are the visitors here. Not the wolves."

With that, I threw the bag of ice in the sink and stormed upstairs to start packing. I yanked my suitcase down out of the top of the guest closet and tossed it on the bed. I pulled my clothes out of the dresser—stopping to gawk at the big black eye that I now sported—and shoved them in the suitcase however I could get them to fit. It was only a moment and Aunt Sissy was standing in the doorway.

"Torie," she said.

I ignored her.

"Torie!"

"What?"

"Your Uncle Joe's only trying to protect what is his. Please, don't go."

"No, I'm going. I have never felt so unwelcome in my whole life, and it has nothing to do with you. I'm clashing with everybody all over the place. It's time for me to leave," I said.

She was quiet a moment while I tried to get my clothes in the suitcase. Somehow, they always fit when I'm leaving for a trip, but they never fit going home. "What did you mean by a minister who was the founder of the city and all that?"

I stopped for a minute and put a hand on my hip. "Anna's parson was none other than the founder of this city. Konrad Nagel," I said.

She shook her head and laughed. "Thus the black eye by his esteemed descendant, Roberta Flagg."

"Yes," I said.

"I can't believe you didn't hit her back," she said and laughed again.

"Well, I almost did, but then I realized that my stepfather wasn't the sheriff here. I'm an outsider. You know, somebody who comes along and rewrites history and wants to save the wolves! Y'all would probably string me up for sure. Throw the book at me and whatever else you could find," I said. "Besides, she was already out the door before I could get up off of the floor."

Aunt Sissy didn't say anything for the longest time while I struggled with shoving my dirty socks in a small trash bag. I exhaled loudly. "I can't believe after you read that diary . . . you know those wolves are probably hers. They're probably the descendants of the very wolves that Anna listened to night after night. And I just don't believe your attitude about it," I said.

"Are you done freaking out?" Aunt Sissy asked.

"I'm done freaking out unless somebody actually shoots one of them. Then you're going to see me all freaked out again. So, I have to leave before it comes to that, because I don't think I'll ever look at my Uncle Joe the same way again."

"I've never known you to quit anything in your life," Aunt Sissy said.

"What? What is that supposed to mean? Have you looked at my eye?"

"Can't help but see it. It sticks out farther than your fore-head," she said.

I crossed my arms and did my best to look menacing with a big purple hunk of flesh bulging below my brow.

"You can't leave. You can't leave until you find out every-thing," she said.

"I have found out everything! Isaac Nagel was killed by his psycho father, the founder of the city—a *hero*—because he was in love with a teenage Swedish girl who never harmed any-body. Then she died in a fire, his baby died in a fire, they killed the wolves. Jesus Christ, Aunt Sissy . . . I found the truth. I found everything. There is nothing left to find."

"Have you been to the cemetery?" she asked.

"What? What cemetery?"

"The Lutheran cemetery. You go there and tell me if you've discovered everything," she said.

"What?"

Aunt Sissy never hesitated as she walked out of the guest room.

"What is that supposed to mean?" I called out after her.

She didn't answer. I went after her.

"Aunt Sissy!"

She turned around halfway down the steps. "What?"

"He can't kill the wolf. Not while I'm here, at least. If you want me to stay, he has to promise not to kill that wolf," I said.

"All right," she said. "I'll talk to him. But you have to go to the cemetery."

"Fine," I said.

It was at that moment that I suddenly realized how much Aunt Sissy reminded me of my boss, Sylvia. Aunt Sissy knew what was in the cemetery already. She knew what I would find, but instead of telling me, she wanted me to go out and find it for myself. I was just a young whippersnapper, after all.

•

I pulled the truck into the parking lot of the Lutheran cemetery in the middle of town. I jumped out and headed through the rusty wrought-iron gates that were connected to the wrought-iron fence that surrounded the entire cemetery. I love old cemeteries. Especially ones with the cool art. In St. Louis the Bellefontaine and Calvary cemeteries have the coolest cemetery art, with large marble statues of angels and the Virgin Mary. And there are some graves that even have life-sized statues of the people that are buried beneath. Kind of creepy, but still cool.

This cemetery had some great art. I passed a statue of an angel bent low and mourning the dead. One angel in the next row was poised, one arm stretched high toward heaven, as if to take flight. Of course, it was the late Victorians who really went all out. Today we could afford the same artwork, but we just don't do it. Prior to about 1880, it was just as rare to find that kind of extravagant artwork as it is today.

As I walked along, I couldn't help but wonder where they buried the dead now. This cemetery was full, looked like it had been full for at least twenty years. I passed by a huge tree in the middle of the cemetery and it made me stop. Anna's words echoed through my head.

As I stand on sacred ground, I vow to thee that we will be together. Soon.

I shivered as I made my way to the older part of the cemetery. There, about ten rows from the last row, was a gigantic monument. It was at least five feet tall. The inscription read:

KONRAD VILHELM NAGEL
19 Sept. 1808–8 Jan. 1859

Beloved father, leader, minister
He has gone home to be with the Lord

There was a blank space between Nagel's grave and the next one. In a cemetery that was packed full, that sort of bothered me. I kept looking around and I found the graves of Karl Bloomquist and his wife, Brigitta. Karl's was to the left of Brigitta's, and his tombstone read that he had died in 1875, at the age of fifty-seven. Brigitta's, of course, read exactly as the death record had read.

And then, all the way against the fence, was Anna's. It did not say *beloved daughter* or *beloved sister*. It simply gave her dates, and that was it. Then, next to hers, was Isaac Nagel's. "Oh my gosh," I said out loud. I wasn't expecting him to be buried next to her. As far as I could tell, everybody who had been involved in this scenario was against them being together. To put them together in death was just touching. Albeit morbidly sad, but still touching.

And if you love me as you have professed all these long winter months, then say that you will be my wife.

Isaac Nagel's tombstone read:

ISAAC KONRAD NAGEL
20 June 1840–10 Jan. 1859

Oh, jeez. I couldn't take much more of this. It was so sad that I could barely stand it anymore. I was ready to go home and forget about Anna Bloomquist and Isaac Nagel and their heartrending story.

Yes, my love. Yes.

And their baby.

Where was little Emelie's tombstone? Most of the time, when a baby and its mother died within a few days of each other, both names went on the same tombstone. Or children were buried together. For instance, my great-grandfather had three stillborns throughout his life, and when he was older and had the money, he bought one tombstone with the names of all three on it. It was not uncommon. It also wasn't uncommon for infants to go without tombstones at all. But since Emelie had died within a few days of her mother, I would have thought her name would have been inscribed on the same stone.

But her name was nowhere on Anna's stone.

I spent the next two hours combing every row of graves, looking for Emelie Bloomquist's stone. It was nowhere.

I had a headache about the size of Montana and a queasy stomach, but I knocked on the door of the church office anyway. Lisa answered the door and gasped when she saw my eye. "Oh, Lord," she said. "I heard about it, but I didn't know it was that bad."

"What?"

"I heard that Roberta decked you over at the grocery," she said. "I had no idea she could hit like that."

"Well, thank you very much," I said.

"Come on in," she said. "What can I do for you?"

"Do you have a plot of the cemetery? You know, something that tells who's buried where," I said.

"Sure," she answered. "Why?"

"Well, there's a baby that died with her mother and she doesn't have a marker," I said. "So, I just wanted to see if she was anywhere on the plot."

"Sure thing," she said. She pulled out a big book that had the graveyard sectioned off into ten areas. "You know, I get genealogists in here all the time. They always seem to be out-of-towners."

"Why do you think that is?"

"I don't know. It's like nobody here cares who the heck they are. It's always the ones who move away and then some-how glamorize their 'prairie frontier' roots," she said. "As if they're going to find a life like *Little House on the Prairie.*"

"Every person who moved out here was living their own version of *Little House on the Prairie,*" I said.

"Whatever. You family history nuts are weird."

"Yes, that's me. The nut that fell off of the family tree." I looked at the book and went through it section by section. There was no plot of land assigned to Emelie Bloomquist. Or even an Emelie Nagel.

"You know, a lot of people just buried their family on their land," Lisa said.

"Yes," I said. "I've come across that a few times. That's ter-rible for a genealogist."

"I bet."

I looked through the book some more and decided to check out that blank space next to Konrad Nagel. The name Isaac Nagel had been written in, and then a line had been drawn through his name. That was peculiar. I don't think I've ever come across anything like that before. "What does this mean?" I asked. "There's a line through his name."

"Oh, well, I'm not sure how they do it in all cemeteries, but in this one, it means that the body was moved."

"Moved?"

"Buried somewhere else. See, there's a few people . . . right there's one," she said, and pointed to another name, "whose families moved their loved ones for whatever reason."

Indeed, there were a few of them throughout the cemetery that had their names crossed out. Isaac Nagel had originally been buried next to his father and then he was moved next to Anna Bloomquist. So who had moved him? And when had he been moved?

"You wouldn't happen to have any Tylenol or Advil?" I asked.

She opened her desk and tossed a bottle at me. "Water fountain's around the corner."

"Thanks," I said. I went to the water fountain and took the pills. It's always a miracle that I don't choke on the pills when I take them with water from a fountain. I can never figure out how to put the pills in my mouth, lean forward to get the water, and keep the pills in the back of my throat.

When I came around the corner, I smiled and waved. "Thanks, Lisa."

"Anytime," she said.

I stepped back outside and stood there for a moment. Then something struck me. The dates on the tombstones. I ran through the cemetery to Konrad Nagel's grave. He had died January 8, 1859. Then I ran to the back of the cemetery and found Isaac's. He had died January 10, 1859. There was no way that Konrad Nagel could have killed Anna's lover and his only son. Konrad had been killed two days before Isaac.

So who killed Konrad?

And who killed Isaac?

I was going to need more than Advil for my head.

Fourteen

Time had gotten away from me. By the time I pulled up in front of the marina, I expected to find Rudy and Colin sitting outside with their fishing gear in their hands and scowls on their faces. Instead, I found an ambulance, a sheriff's car, and a coroner. I had barely stopped the truck when I threw the door open and jumped out. I ran inside the marina as fast as I could, heart thudding with an adrenaline boost.

"Torie," Rudy said and grabbed me by the arm. "Am I glad to see you."

"What is going on?"

"What happened to your eye?" he asked.

"Oh, Roberta punched me."

He just stared at me for a minute and then he shook his head. He looked as if he'd eaten something that didn't agree with him. As if he were ready to puke at any moment. "Somebody killed Brian Bloomquist."

"What?" I asked. "Why? How?"

Rudy seemed to be a little pasty, too. "I don't know why, but the how . . . Seems to be a knife in the jugular."

I gasped. "Oh, no," I said, and covered my mouth.

"That's not the worst of it," he said and hugged me.

"What? What else could be worse?" Suddenly I realized that Colin was nowhere around. "Oh, no. Not Colin." All I could think about was my mother's happiness shattering into a million pieces. She'd spent so many years alone and all of a sudden she had found this man who made her really happy, and then I had to take him to Minnesota and get him killed.

"Colin's fine," Rudy said. "Well, sort of."

"What, Rudy? What?"

Rudy moved aside so that I could get a good view of my stepfather.

In handcuffs.

Colin was being questioned by the local sheriff. Blood covered his hands, was smeared on the front of his shirt and all over his shoes. He wore a very worried expression on his face, but the worry seemed to be wrestling with anger. I could see it seething from his very being.

"Colin killed Brian Bloomquist?"

"No," Rudy said. "Of course he didn't kill Brian Bloomquist."

"Well, then *why* is he in handcuffs?"

"Because they *think* he killed him."

"I am so confused, I'm amazed my head hasn't exploded all over the place. Like those watermelons when that comedian Gallagher gets ahold of them."

"You look like shit," he said. "Sorry, but it's the truth."

I just smiled at him. No sympathy. No worry. Just you look like shit. Well, he didn't look too hot himself. It made me worry about what he'd seen. "Okay, slow down and tell me everything," I said.

He took a deep, cleansing breath, looked to the sky as if for guidance, and began talking. "Colin and I came back in from the lake about five-thirty. That's a little later than Brian likes, but at the last minute I got a really good bite," he said.

"Just tell me how my stepfather ended up in handcuffs!"

"I'm trying, Torie. Be patient. I went to the men's room, which is around back. So if you have to take a whiz, you don't have to come all the way in the building. Colin came on in to settle up with Brian and buy some new fishing line. When I got out of the men's room, I came into the store, and there was Colin standing over the body with the knife in his hand and blood everywhere," he said. "I mean, two seconds later the authorities came in behind me and—"

"Which means somebody either heard something or saw something . . . or Brian managed to dial 911," I said.

"Yeah, that's what I figured, too. But anyway, the authorities came in and—"

"There has to be an explanation for this," I said and rubbed my forehead. I forgot all about my black eye until my fingers rubbed over the side of my head. Even my temple hurt. I winced.

This wasn't looking like a much better scenario for my mother's happiness, either. How happy could she be if her beloved husband was rotting behind bars for all of eternity? I had to get some answers. What was I going to tell her? I had to call her on the phone and tell her . . . but what exactly? I grabbed a deputy as he went by. "Excuse me. That's my stepfather. Can I speak to somebody about what's going on?"

The deputy was blond and blue-eyed, so Aryan that Hitler

would have snatched him in a second. "Sure, just a minute, ma'am."

I hate it when people younger than me call me ma'am. It makes me feel so old. I tapped my foot and crossed my arms, chomping at the bit. All the while, there were people snapping pictures and measuring things. Blood splatters or something. The body was gone, but on the floor I could see the tape where it had outlined him. And the blood. Wasn't the first time I'd seen copious amounts of human blood, but it still unnerved me. I didn't puke this time, but every time a flash went off, it made my gut contract. The blood looked electric in the flash of the camera.

I tried to look away, but bumped into somebody. There were more people crammed in that store than needed to be, and I was getting a serious case of weirded-out claustrophobia.

The sheriff walked over to me and introduced himself. "Hi, I'm Sheriff Aberg," he said. "I understand you're the stepdaughter of Mr. Brooke."

"Yes," I said. "He's a sheriff, too."

"So I understand."

"Can you tell me what's going on? My mother is going to be worried sick. I need to tell her something . . . solid. No hot air."

Sheriff Aberg was about my age, with wide-set green eyes and red hair. He kept his notebook out, but stuck his thumb behind the buckle of his belt. "All right," he said. "Your step-father says he came in and found the body lying in a puddle of blood and a knife sticking out of his neck."

I shook my head in disbelief. I already knew what he was going to tell me. "So he took the knife out of Mr. Bloomquist's neck," I said. "Didn't he?"

Sheriff Aberg nodded. "Said he thought he might be able to save Brian. Evidently Mr. Bloomquist was still gurgling when your stepfather got in here."

"Aw, Jeeee-sus," I said and hugged myself close. I didn't need to know that. I swallowed hard. "So, why is he in hand-cuffs?"

"Please, Mrs. . . . ?"

"O'Shea. Torie. Well, my real name is Victory O'Shea."

"Mrs. O'Shea, he's from out of town. He's been seen in here every day for a few days in a row. I can't be so sure that he hasn't been scoping the place out and this wasn't an intended robbery."

"A robbery?" I asked. "Does he have any money on him? Don't you usually get the money first and then kill the clerk?"

"I wouldn't know," Sheriff Aberg said. "I have never robbed anybody."

Okay, take a deep breath. "Why would he rob a man with-out any gloves on, no ski mask? And wouldn't you think he'd use a gun? I mean, there has to be a . . . *neater* way of robbing somebody. People are going to notice somebody fleeing from a crime scene with blood all over him," I said. "He's a sheriff, for crying out loud. He would have thought of these things!"

"Just calm down, Mrs. O'Shea," he said. "This is just a pre-liminary investigation."

"Then why is he in handcuffs?"

He looked around the room and shifted his weight to the other foot. "He got a little . . ."

"Oh, no."

"Yeah, he got a little physical when he realized he was standing over a dead man with the murder weapon and three deputies had guns pointed at him. It's a miracle he didn't get shot," he said. "Actually, one of my deputies did shoot off a couple of rounds at him but he ducked and rolled and managed to miss any bullets."

"Oh . . . I . . . I am just speechless," I said.

Stupid, stupid idiot.

"So, I'm taking him in," he said. "At least until we've processed everything here."

"How long will that take?" I asked, the hysteria rising in my voice.

"Just calm down," he said.

"I am calm," I said through clenched teeth.

"You can come down to the station with us," he said.

"Can I talk to him?"

"Not yet," he said.

"Well . . . well, do you have any other suspects?"

"Mrs. O'Shea—"

"Okay, I know. Time. It will take time," I said. I looked up at Rudy, who was looking pretty helpless at the moment.

"Oh, and your husband will have to come with us, too."

"*What?* Why?"

"He had just come in the building when our deputies got here. Damn near got himself shot, too. He's a witness," Sheriff Aberg said.

The sheriff left me standing there next to Rudy, who was looking pretty pale at the moment. "You . . . you almost got shot?"

"I hit the deck, crawled under a shelf, and covered my head," he said. He shrugged like it was nothing, but I could see him shaking and the skin around his mouth was white as a ghost.

"Oh, why didn't you tell me?" I asked. I hugged him as close to me as I could. He hugged me back so hard it took my breath away. "Are you okay?"

"I can't seem to stop shaking," he said. "But otherwise I'm fine."

"I can't believe you didn't tell me," I said. He shook so hard it was as if he were having convulsions.

"You didn't give me a chance," he said.

"I am so sorry," I said.

"I'm just glad it's over. It took about seven seconds for those three bullets to fly around the room, but it felt like seven hours," he said.

The crowd started moving, and two deputies walked toward us with Colin in handcuffs. As he came toward us, he looked straight at me. He didn't look at Rudy. He didn't look at anything except my eyes. And then with the most determined expression I've ever seen, he said, "Get me out of this. Do you understand?"

I nodded.

As they led him out of the door, he looked back over his shoulder at me and yelled, "I didn't do this, Torie! Tell Jalena I love her."

"Oh, my God," I said.

"What?" Rudy asked.

"I have to call my mother."

"Mr. O'Shea," Sheriff Aberg said. "You have to come with me. Mrs. O'Shea, you can follow in your vehicle."

Fifteen

It was hours before I could see Colin. I still hadn't called my
mother. I just couldn't bring myself to call her until I had
more information. She would ask questions that I didn't have
answers to, so why call her? Okay, all right, a part of me just
couldn't do it.

When they finally took me back to the interrogation room,
my knees were knocking, my hands sweating. I don't know
why. Maybe it was just because it suddenly sank in that this
was no joke. My stepfather was in handcuffs and could be
charged with murder if they didn't find the truth. On top of
all the personal reasons why this was a bad thing, in the back
of my mind I kept thinking, *New Kassel is going to have to elect
a new sheriff.* It was an odd thing to intrude on my thoughts,
but it was there nonetheless.

They sat me down across from him in a room far too cold
and far too sterile, and for the first time in all the years that
I've known Colin, two things happened. He actually looked

glad to see me and I actually felt sorry for him.

"You stupid idiot," I said to him.

"I know, I know," he said.

"You had three guns pointed at you! Why did you try to run?"

He was quiet a moment. "I don't know. I panicked. For the first time in my life I know how the other guy feels. I looked up, saw those guns pointed at me, and I knew what they thought. I knew they thought I killed him," he said. "It's that old flight-or-fight thing."

"No, no, no. Flight, fight, or do nothing," I said. "Do nothing is the answer you're looking for here. That's what you should have done. I can't believe you tried to run."

"Gun pointed at me. Me run," he said. "It's instinct."

"Remember that next time you have a gun on a suspect," I said.

"If there is a next time," he said. He tried to stretch, but the handcuffs kept him from entirely doing so. Colin and I go back a long way. Basically, he's always interfering with the things that I do, and I'm always interfering with his investigations. He's arrested me a few times. Then he went and married my mother. But the bottom line is he's a good guy at heart and my mother adores him. And New Kassel could do a lot worse than Colin Brooke as sheriff. I didn't even want to imagine who would take his place.

"Okay, so what next? Have you called a lawyer? Are they booking you?" I asked.

A puzzled expression crossed his face. "What happened to your eye?"

"Oh, I got punched by a local. There are some pretty intense people around here. But enough about that. You better be telling me exactly what happened and what I have to do to get you out of here," I said.

"Does it hurt?" he asked.

"Yes," I said.

"Good," he said, and then laughed. I laughed along with him for a moment before my irritation with him brought me to my senses.

"Colin," I said. "What do I do?"

"I don't think they're going to actually file charges. Yet," he said. "I think there's enough doubt in their minds—probably because I'm in law enforcement—that they're going to wait for some preliminary forensics before they go booking me and what have you. I think they have thirty-six hours or such before they have to book me."

"Okay."

"So that gives you enough time to find out who did this," he said.

I just blinked at him.

"What?" he asked.

"You want me to . . . You want me to what?"

"To find out who did this, so you can get me out of here," he said.

"Colin, I am not a cop."

"Well, that has certainly never stopped you before," he said.

"No, no, no, wait. Th-this is way out of my league," I said. "This has nothing to do with estates and wills and old, long-forgotten dead things."

"How do you know?" he asked.

"Colin, I am not equipped to solve regular homicides or . . . a robbery."

"This was no robbery," he said. "This was either vengeance or a wipeout."

"A wipeout?"

"Yeah, somebody wanted him out of the picture and wiped him out. The question is, what picture would that be?" he said.

"Colin—"

"Help me, Torie," he said. "You're my only hope."

I couldn't help it. I laughed. And it wasn't just a snicker. It was a full-fledged rear your head back and belly laugh. I'm sure part of it was due to nerves and adrenaline.

"What?" he said. "I'm on my hands and knees here and you're laughing."

"No, it's just, you know. You reminded me of Princess Leia. 'Help me, Obi Wan Kenobi.' "

"Can you be serious?" he asked.

"No," I said. "No, I can't be serious. This is preposterous. *You* need to be serious. You need to get a good lawyer and hire a private eye."

He pinched the bridge of his nose and looked at me with bleary eyes. "When I got into the store, he was . . . he was trying to crawl toward the phone. The knife was sticking out of his neck. He tried to talk, but I think his voice box—his wound—it was too severe. He mouthed something to me," he said.

"What was it?"

"I'm not sure."

"Think. Try."

"I am," he said. His eyes clouded with the memory of what he had witnessed. An atrocious memory that he would file with all the other atrocious things that he had witnessed as a sheriff. "I'm pretty sure he said 'B-12'."

"B-12? Like the vitamin?"

"Yes," he said. "I know it doesn't make any sense, but I'm almost positive that is what he said."

"That's it? Was there anybody else in the room?"

"No," he said.

"What about . . . You said he was crawling toward the phone? So he hadn't made it to the phone yet?" I asked.

"That's right."

"So, who called 911?" I asked.

"I don't know," he said.

"How much time passed between the time you found him, you pulled the knife out, and the authorities came in?" I asked.

"Oh, like, seconds. I saw his legs behind the counter, I ran around the counter, immediately realized that the only way he could be saved was to take the knife out and put pressure on the wound. I pulled the knife out, was getting ready to take my shirt off to hold against the wound, because I couldn't find anything else, when Rudy came in. I was going to have Rudy call 911 when he came in, because I knew he was right behind me. It would only take him a minute to use the toilet. Anyway, I looked up at Rudy, then the deputies burst through. I panicked."

"Lord," I said. "That's not a lot of time to play with. So somebody either had to have come into the store and seen him there before you came in, or else the killer dialed the police from his cell phone or something. How else did the sheriff know that somebody had been stabbed at the marina?"

"Okay . . . ?" he said.

"Which means, if somebody came in and saw him before you came in, then that person can verify that you weren't in there stabbing Mr. Bloomquist in the throat," I said. "Maybe we don't have to solve who did the murder. Maybe we just need to find a witness who can prove that you didn't."

He sighed. "Well, that's encouraging," he said.

I reached across the table and squeezed Colin's hand. "I'll do everything I can to get you out of here," I said. "All right?"

He nodded. "You look like shit," he said.

"That's all right," I said. "*You* just asked for *my* help. The world is mine for the taking."

"That's not funny," he said.

"Yes, it is."

"I could be going up the river for life," he said.

A vision of my mother's face, shattered by her husband going up the river for life.

"Okay, you're right. That was uncalled for," I said. "Try not to worry."

"Right," he said.

I stood up to leave. "I'll bring you a cheeseburger or something," I said.

"Better make it three. I might be here awhile," he said.

The esteemed Sheriff Simon Aberg made me wait two hours before I could talk with him again. But I suppose that was all right, since Rudy had to be "officially" questioned and I would have had to wait for that as well. I called my Aunt Sissy and told her what had happened. She'd already heard about Brian, but had no idea that we were involved in any way. I think she was beginning to reevaluate her invitation to us.

It was eight P.M. and my stomach was grumbling, my head felt like it had suddenly split in two and started growing in different directions, and I was just downright ticked off. Finally, the sheriff came out and motioned for me to enter his office of white ceramic tile. As I entered his office, all I could think was, *So this is what an igloo looks like from the inside.*

"What happened to your eye?" he said, and motioned to a lawn chair. It must have been the expression on my face that caused him to explain. "Some guy bled all over the other one and I had to get rid of it. I'm waiting for my replacement chair. Have a seat."

I sat down.

He gave me a raised eyebrow. "The eye?"

"Oh, Roberta Flagg punched me," I said.

"She did?"

"Yeah," I said. "I said something less than glowing about one of her ancestors."

"Oh," he said. "Bad move."

I just nodded.

"Want to press charges?"

"No," I said. "No, that's not necessary."

"What are you guys doing up here from Missouri, anyway?"

"Visiting my aunt. And the guys were fishing," I said.

He sucked his teeth, as if he'd eaten corn on the cob for lunch. "So, what did you want to see me about?"

"Look, I know you can't share the specifics with me about the case," I said. "But, I was wondering . . . today . . . who . . . how did you find out that somebody had been murdered at the marina? Was there a 911 call?"

He sighed. "Why?" Then he tapped his pencil on his desk.

"Because if whoever called 911 actually saw a body lying in a pool of its own blood, with the knife sticking out of its neck, and my stepfather was nowhere around, then I'd think you'd have a tough time continuing to believe that my stepfather killed him," I said, as calmly as I could manage.

He seemed to acquiesce, even if only his mind. I could see it on his face. "I'll check into it."

"Good," I said. "That's all I ask."

"Does it hurt?" he asked and pointed to my head.

"Yes," I said. "I think I'm getting just a small taste of what it feels like to be the elephant man. My head actually feels heavier on this side."

He tapped his pencil again.

"I'm sure it will feel better tomorrow," I said.

He snickered.

"Also . . . I know this probably has nothing to do with the case, but I actually spoke to Mr. Bloomquist earlier in the day," I said.

"Really?"

"Yes. I went out on the lake with the guys for the morning and then they brought me back at lunchtime and I went . . . I went and did some sightseeing," I said. "But before I left, I talked to Mr. Bloomquist."

"What about?"

"Well, his family tree, actually. See, I'm a genealogist and I work for the historical society for Granite County, Missouri," I said. "And, well, it's a long convoluted story about why I was speaking to him, but when I first approached him, he wasn't sure who I was or what I wanted. He said something odd."

"What was that?"

"He said, 'You can tell Kimberly Canton my answer is still no.' Do you have any idea who Kimberly Canton is, or what he was referring to?" I asked.

His expression dropped. "Real estate developer," he said. "She's been trying to get everybody to sell their lakefront property."

"Oh."

"I think she's trying to find a good-sized lake, upstate a ways, that she can monopolize. You know, go in and just turn the whole thing into a resort. But she'd have to have a one-hundred percent buyout. Or at least close to it," he said. "She's been after Brian to sell that marina for a long time. She wants my measly five acres, too. Some of us have sold, some of us are still holding out."

"How much does Brian own?"

"I think he's got thirty acres or so altogether. Hell, some people own as much as a hundred or so acres, not all of it shore, you understand, but still land that connects to the lake," he said. "It's big now. Up on Superior, if your family bought land fifty or so years ago, you'd be a millionaire today."

"Wow," I said.

"Now, Olin Lake isn't quite as prime as Superior," he said. "But it's still choice land nonetheless. It'd make a nice little resort town, don't you think?"

"Well—"

"Some people think so. There's a lot of pressure to sell. Olin would suddenly be on the map, so to speak," he said. "I mean, fishing season already brings a horde of tourists and fisherman. But nothing like it would be if it was a resort town. What I can't get people to understand is that if one person, Ms. Canton, owns it all, then it's profit for Ms. Canton, not the town of Olin. Or any of its people."

"I understand. The town I live in is a tourist town. But all of the townsfolk own their own businesses. We work together as a town, but if business is good, it's good for the individual, not one big corporation."

"Exactly," he said. "That's what I—and the mayor—have been trying to tell people."

"Well, that's interesting. You think you need to question Ms. Canton? I mean, Brian seemed pretty irritated when he thought she'd sent me. Maybe there's something to it," I said.

"Maybe," he said. "Thanks for the tip."

"All right," I said. I wrote down Aunt Sissy's phone number and my cell-phone number. "This is where you can reach me. If anything should develop where my stepfather is concerned."

"Thank you," he said. "Have a nice evening, Mrs. O'Shea."

"You, too, Sheriff."

Sixteen

My head hurt a lot worse the next morning. It wasn't quite as swollen, but all of my movements seemed to feel as though they were happening ten seconds after I commanded them to move. I rolled over, bunching all of the blankets up as I went, to find Rudy staring at the ceiling. "You all right?" I asked.

"Couldn't sleep," he said.

I kissed him and laid my head on his chest. "As lame as it sounds, all I can say is it will go away. The vision of . . . it. The blood. Believe me, I know."

"Yeah, I know you know. Now I'm wondering if I've been an insensitive jerk to you," he said.

I giggled. "A jerk sometimes. Insensitive sometimes, but never the two together."

"Thanks."

"I'm joking," I said. "You're my rock. Always have been."

We lay there a few more minutes until we smelled breakfast

cooking. "You know, I could get used to this. Having breakfast ready when I wake up," I said.

"Yeah," he said.

"But it ain't going to happen," I said.

"No," Rudy said. "You gonna call your mom?"

"Yes," I said.

"When?"

"After breakfast," I said.

"Well, let's go eat so you can call her," he said.

"Oh, yeah, can't wait."

We fumbled our way out of bed, down the stairs, and into the kitchen. I let my nose be my guide, since at least one of my eyes wasn't seeing too well.

"Oh, you look like hell," Aunt Sissy said when I came into the room.

"Thanks," I said.

"You don't look too hot, either," she said to Rudy. She put his coffee down in front of him.

"Where's Uncle Joe?" I asked.

"He's outside getting ready to work on that shelter," she said. "He could use a hand today, if you're not going to be out on the lake today, Rudy."

"No, I'm not going to be fishing today," he said. "Probably won't fish again until I'm safe and sound in my own state. I'd be happy to help Uncle Joe with the shelter."

"Good," she said.

Aunt Sissy put the food on the table. I tried to eat with my head propped on one hand. Don't ask. It just felt better that way. We were all quiet, just shoveling the food in. Nobody had anything important to say, and we all felt stupid for making idle chitchat. So we just said nothing.

Finally, I broke the silence. "Is there somebody other than Roberta Flagg who works at the historical society?" I asked.

"Why?" Aunt Sissy asked.

"Because I'd like to get back in there and look at some things, but I really don't want to run the risk of ticking off Miss Minnesota Boxing Champion," I said.

"Yeah," she said. "You'll have to go tomorrow. It's the only day other than Sunday that she takes off. She has Tiny Holmann watch things for her."

"Great," I said. "Then I'll go to the library today. The one in Cedar Springs. You can take me there. Right?"

"Yes," she said. "So did you make it to the cemetery?"

"Yeah," I said.

She glanced at Rudy.

"He knows everything," I said.

"Oh," she said.

"How did you know?" I asked.

"How did I know what?" she countered.

"That Konrad Nagel couldn't have killed his son? When did you have a chance to check it out? You didn't even know Konrad's name. You couldn't have figured it out before me," I said.

"I didn't," she said. "I have no idea what you're talking about."

"Then why did you send me to the cemetery?"

"Because of Emelie. I had to deliver a tree to the Catholic church in town. I got to thinking that now that I had a name to go with this story . . . Anna Bloomquist . . . maybe I could find where she was buried. You know, something tangible. I wanted to see it for myself."

"I certainly understand that," I said.

"Boy, does she," Rudy added.

"And so I went to the Lutheran church, went out into the graveyard, and found Anna's grave. And I found her parents' graves. But I could never find the grave for her daughter, Emelie. No marker, nothing," she said.

"I noticed that, too."

Aunt Sissy got up and began putting the dirty dishes in the dishwasher. She talked while she piled them in. "So, all the way home I kept thinking, Where is little Emelie?"

Silence hung in the air.

"Where do you think little Emelie is?" Rudy asked.

She shut the door to the dishwasher and looked at me. "I don't know. I was hoping Torie could tell me that. It's not the end of the story until I know where Emelie Bloomquist is. If she's buried here on this property, instead of a cemetery, then I want to know where the grave is. I want to put a marker up. If she's not . . ."

"If she's not, what?"

"I don't know. If she's not buried in the cemetery with her parents and she's not buried here, then where is she?"

"Oh, jeez," I said. "Again, Aunt Sissy, we may never know the answer to that question."

"I don't care. I want to try," she said.

"All right," I said, holding up a hand in surrender. "I noticed that Sven is not buried at the Lutheran cemetery, either. Maybe there's a family plot somewhere else. Like, like the cousins that they lived with when they first moved down here," I suggested.

"The ones in the census? That Karl and Sven lived with after the fire?"

"Right," I said. "Maybe they have a family plot on their

property. I need to look at the land records and find out where their property would have been. And who knows, if Sven isn't buried here in Olin, maybe he moved to one of the neighboring towns. Maybe she's buried there."

"Yeah, but why would Sven wait years to bury his niece?" Rudy asked.

"Maybe he didn't, maybe he did. Maybe he just had her moved. Hell, I don't know," I said. "I'm just throwing out ideas. He seems to be the one that had the conscience in the family. He reported the deaths in the first place. He's the one who convinced Anna to live, for the baby's sake. He's the one who took Anna to Cedar Springs to have Emelie baptized—"

I stopped.

Aunt Sissy and I both looked at each other. We had the same thought.

"Maybe he buried her at that Lutheran church in Cedar Springs, for the same reason that they baptized her there," I said.

"That's an idea," Aunt Sissy said.

"Yes, but separating mother and daughter?" Rudy asked.

"If Sven thought some harm would come to her grave or something . . . you know, because of a prejudice. He might have felt it was worth separating them. Or maybe he buried her there simply because she was baptized there and the people didn't have the ill feelings that the church in Olin had. I honestly don't know. She may not even be in Cedar Springs. It's just an idea. Either way, I'm going to check out some of the records in Cedar Springs."

"So what do you think happened to Sven? If he's not buried here, he must have moved," Rudy said.

"Yes, but keep in mind that he could just as easily be buried on his land, wherever that is. We know it's not here, because by 1861 it belonged to the Rogers family. Or he could have died on a trip somewhere . . . Just because he's not at the church cemetery doesn't mean he didn't live here. But if he's got descendants here—Brian Bloomquist was one of them—it's safe to say he didn't go too far," I said.

"So, what was this about Konrad Nagel?" Aunt Sissy asked.

"Well, you know how Anna says in her diary that the parson killed her lover, which we now know is Isaac Nagel, the parson's son," I said.

"Yes."

"Well, Konrad couldn't have killed Isaac."

"Why not?"

"Because Konrad was murdered two days before Isaac was killed," I said. "There's no way."

Aunt Sissy looked out her kitchen window a moment. "Did they ever find out who killed Konrad?"

"Well, I haven't been able to get my hands on any real documents, newspaper clippings or anything. According to Roberta, he was killed by a stranger who had come to town and needed a place to stay. Parson Nagel let him stay at his home and the stranger killed him in the middle of the night."

"So I've heard," Aunt Sissy said. "I mean, we've all heard the story vaguely."

"What's bothering you?" I asked, noticing that her eyes were seeing something beyond the here and now.

"I'm just wondering if the same person who killed the parson turned around and killed his son Isaac two days later," she said.

"I don't know," I said. "I don't know if we'll ever know. One thing's for sure, though."

"What?" Rudy asked.

"I don't think it was a stranger that killed the parson. Not if he killed Isaac, too."

"Why?" Rudy asked.

"Because why would a perfect stranger kill a parson and then lurk nearby and kill the parson's son two days later? I mean, that seems more like a personal vendetta," I said.

"I agree," Rudy said.

"Or unless Isaac was a witness to the first murder, and the killer wanted him dead so there would be no case against him," Aunt Sissy said.

"Yes, but whoever killed Isaac hung him in a barn for everybody to see. Not only did he hang Isaac in a barn, he hung Isaac in Anna Bloomquist's barn," I said. "Why would he do that if he was trying to erase a witness?"

Rudy and Aunt Sissy both chewed on that for a minute. My mind reeled, and that just added to the pain I was already feeling. "Do you have some Advil or something?"

"Yes," Aunt Sissy said. "How many do you want?"

"As many as you can give me that will equal a prescription dose," I said.

"Man," Rudy said and shook his head.

"What?" I asked.

"I want to come with you guys today, instead of building a shelter," he said. "This is fascinating."

"Now you know how I become so obsessed so easily," I said.

"Amazing," he said. "You just think of the olden days as days filled with going to church, plowing fields, warding off disease, plowing fields, going to church. I mean, you don't think of the past as being personal. You know, that those people did exactly what we do every day, loved their spouses, their kids, and life, just like us."

"Yeah," I said. "It's easy to depersonalize the past."

"You have to call your mother," he said.

I sighed. "Give me the phone."

Rudy gave me the phone and I dialed it as Aunt Sissy came back into the room with her palm full of Advil and handed me a big glass of water. I swallowed four of them just as my mother answered the phone.

"Hi, Mom," I said.

"Hello," she said. "It's early. Something wrong?"

"Well, yeah," I said. "How are the kids?"

"Getting ready for school," she said. "I keep telling Rachel that if she keeps looking at herself in the mirror she's going to grow a mustache. She doesn't believe me. What's wrong? Why are you calling?"

"Well, Mom. Colin's all right," I said.

"Oh, nothing ever ends well that starts like that."

"No, seriously, he's fine. But he's sorta been arrested."

"Is that all? You've been arrested twice. What's the problem?" she asked.

"He's been arrested for murder."

It was quiet on the other end of the line and then she just burst into laughter. I let her have her laugh because I knew she wouldn't be laughing later. "You've got to be kidding. Come on," she said.

"No, I'm not kidding. He's been arrested for murder. They will probably bring charges against him today, unless this one lead turns things in his favor," I said.

Her voice changed. No nonsense. Serious. "What happened?"

"Somebody killed the owner of the marina that he and Rudy were fishing at. Colin was found holding the knife. He was just trying to save the guy," I assured her. "But he's from out of town and they aren't looking at it that way."

"He's a sheriff, for crying out loud. He doesn't kill people. He stops people who kill people," she said.

"Well, I know that. And you know that. But law enforcement officers have been known to murder people on occasion. I suppose, since he was holding the murder weapon, they want to make sure he's not one of those hideous few," I said.

"I don't believe this. He goes fishing and gets arrested. How is that possible?" she asked. Before I could answer she answered. "I'll tell you how. He's with you. I have never in all my life seen anybody who has a little black cloud following them around like you do. What is wrong with you, Torie?"

"Well, gee, thanks, Mom."

"You need to see somebody," she said. "A shrink. No, a medium. An exorcist."

"Mother!"

"I just don't believe this," she said. She took a deep breath. "Call me when you find out something. And tell my husband to call me as soon as they allow him a phone call."

I didn't tell her that he could have called her last night. That would probably have sent her over the edge. I just said all right. "Tell the kids to be good. I love you, Mom."

I guess she was weighing how much she loved me or not. Finally, she said, "I love you, too. Hurry." And she hung up.

"Well?" Rudy asked.

"She took it well."

Seventeen

Aunt Sissy and I headed out of Olin to Cedar Springs in the noisy beast she called a truck. Aunt Sissy was quieter than normal, I think, due to the fact that nothing was turning out as she expected. Her investigation of the antiquated document had had a domino effect. Me getting punched in the eye was part of that effect. I really think she had thought that I would just read the diary, look up a few records, and know all the answers about everything, and nobody would be the wiser. Except her. And me. Well, that's rarely the case with anything. As I have found out in the past.

We were about six miles outside of Olin. The trillium was in bloom all along the floor of the forest and I could see the occasional white blossoms from the cab of the truck. The trees were tall and thin trunked, lots of birch and poplar, and of course the evergreens. All of a sudden Aunt Sissy slammed on the brakes and I instantly whipped my head around to see what had caused her to react so abruptly.

About three hundred yards in front of us was a wolf.

"Oh, my God," I said.

"I don't believe it," she said in a controlled voice.

"What's it doing?" I whispered.

"It's carrying roadkill off of the road."

"Ooooh, gross," I said. I could have gone all day without knowing that. Just as Aunt Sissy said it, though, the wolf looked up and right at us.

"It's fresh roadkill. Looks like a deer," she whispered. "This . . . I never thought I'd live to see the day."

The wolf considered its options. Abandon the roadkill or finish its task. She decided to finish her task. I guess humans in a big metal thing didn't seem so intimidating. Or maybe her empty stomach took precedence.

"Why are we whispering?" I asked.

"Hell, I don't know. You started it," she said in a regular voice.

Just as the gray wolf got the deer to the edge of the road, two impossibly little heads peeked out from the bush. The wolf turned and chastised them. What was wrong with them? Somebody would see them. Get back where they were supposed to be. I could imagine every word. Because it was universal. It was exactly what I would have said to my young.

"She's got cubs," I stated plainly.

"No shit, Sherlock."

"You can't kill this wolf," I said.

"I'm not going to kill anything. Except maybe you if you don't stop telling me what I can and can't do."

"You will be just as responsible if you just stand by and let somebody else kill her."

"Shut up already," she said.

"Isn't there like a Crocodile Hunter for wolves or something? You know, call somebody and have them relocated?"

"I don't know," she said.

"You can't—"

"I said, I don't know," Aunt Sissy said. "I'll check into it."

I watched the wolf struggle to drag the carcass into the bush and felt sorry for her. I flashed on a memory of me trying to get my groceries in the house, the bag ripping, Mary running through the mud in her new white tennis shoes, Matthew screaming because he thought I was leaving him in the car. I could relate. The wolf's husband should have helped her carry their groceries. I couldn't help but wonder where he was. It's not like he had an office or a day job.

Once the deer was off the road, Aunt Sissy crept by at about fifteen miles an hour, I guess in case one of the little ones jumped out on the road. I stared after them as long as I could, until the road wound in a sharp turn so that I no longer could keep them in my line of sight.

And then I just sat there listening to the *squeegee, squeegee, squeegee* of the truck with my skin tingling.

We rode along in our own little worlds. Finally, we came to a four-way stop on an open road. I could see for miles in either direction. Another truck sped down the road toward us from the opposite way. Aunt Sissy didn't go. She just waited for the other truck. It was obvious the two drivers knew each other.

"Tom!" she said.

The driver of the other truck pulled up alongside us so that his driver's window was even with ours. "Hello, Sissy," he said. "How ya been?"

"Can't complain," she said. "This is my niece, Torie O'Shea. The one I told you about."

He waved at me. He was a good-sized man from what I could see. About sixty-five or seventy years old, with a bulbous nose and a head full of thick blondish white hair. At least what I could see of his hair. He wore a cap that read *Husband. Dad. Grandpa. Mayor.*

"This is Tom Hujinak," Aunt Sissy said to me. "The mayor."

I waved back and he gave me a toothy grin.

"My niece was wondering if she could talk with you," Sissy said.

"What about?" he asked. He checked his rearview mirror to see if anybody was coming. I turned around in the seat and did the same. All clear.

"She wants to ask you about our house. You know, your house," she said.

"All right," he said. "I was born there. I should be able to tell you something."

"Well, not now," Aunt Sissy said. "Can she come by your office later?"

"Sure. I'll be there until five," he said. "Unless I go fishing. Hey, is she related to the guy who's in jail?"

"Uh . . . yeah," Aunt Sissy said.

He nodded. "All right. Better get off the road. See you later, then," he said.

Aunt Sissy and I both waved and he waved and we drove on in opposite directions. After a moment Aunt Sissy said, "I could have called him and asked him that. I wanted to stall him."

"Why?"

"Because he's gonna drive right by the spot in the road where the wolves were. I wanted to make sure that they had time to get safely into the woods," she said.

I smiled.

Silence for a beat. "How far is Cedar Springs?"

"Oh, we should be coming up on Cedar Springs in about a minute. Biggest town in the county," she said. "It's a happening place."

About a minute later, we drove into town and passed a sign that read CEDAR SPRINGS: POPULATION 10,647. Fast-food joints trimmed the main thoroughfare like a string of brightly lit and colorful beads. McDonald's, Burger King, Subway, and so forth. At least there would be no shortage of places to stop for lunch. The Cedar Springs High School sat on the left. Home of the Cubs. I smiled at that.

Aunt Sissy maneuvered her way through town easily. "Where you want to go first?" she asked. "The library or the courthouse?"

"Oh, uh . . . whichever's the closest. Whichever is the easiest for you," I said.

"Hate it when people won't tell me what they want," she mumbled.

She waved at somebody out in front of Will's Feed and Seed and he waved back. Two turns, through a stop sign, and finally she pulled up in front of the courthouse. It was an old-fashioned courthouse, the kind that sat in the middle of a town square and had a clock and a bell tower on top of it. A monument to past wars stood proudly in the front courtyard. It boasted the names of all the people from this county who had served in World War I, World War II, Korea, Vietnam, and the Gulf War. I was surprised that it didn't list all of the Civil War veterans. Turned out they were all listed in the main hall of the courthouse. That was a pretty good clue as to how old the building was. More than likely it was built when the Civil

War was still fairly fresh in everybody's minds and World War I had yet to happen.

"Okay, what do you need?"

"Uh, court records. You know, for murders."

"Right," she said. She made a turn and went down a flight of stairs until we stood at the one and only door on the lower level.

A few minutes later a clerk had ushered us into a room devoid of windows and natural light, full of dust, books, files, and more dust. I set my purse and my tablet on top of a filing cabinet and turned and looked at the books. I pulled out the one with the appropriate dates and turned to January 1859.

"What will this tell you?" Aunt Sissy said.

"It will only tell me something if charges were actually brought against somebody. You know, if there was an actual court case. Otherwise, it will tell us nothing."

"Oh," she said.

A few seconds went by. "I don't see anything."

"Maybe whoever it was went to court years later," she said.

"Then I'd have to know when that was to look it up. Otherwise, I could be standing here scanning each entry for a forty-year span," I said.

"Great," she said.

"Maybe I should have checked the newspapers first," I said.

"See, I asked you which you wanted to do first, but you wouldn't answer," she said.

I just rolled my eyes.

"Well, what else can we do here?" she asked.

"We can check marriages and land records," I said. "I know Roberta's got land records at the historical society, too, but it won't hurt to look at what I need here."

"All right," she said. "That's upstairs."

•

"What land records are you looking for?" Aunt Sissy said.

"I'm trying to figure out where Sven relocated, because then we might be able to figure out the area that Emelie Bloomquist is buried in."

"Ahh, I see," she said. I pulled out the land records book and began to look by year. I figured that if Karl Bloomquist hadn't died until later, he most likely had bought a new farm after the fire and the death of his wife and daughter. He was living with his cousins, the Hagglund family, in 1860 and sold his property to James Rogers in 1861. So I checked 1861 and 1862 to see if he had bought a new farm.

"Yes," I said. "Karl bought land in this county in 1861 in the Poplar Creek bottom. Do you know where that is?"

"Mmm, I think it used to run right through Cedar Springs. But the creek dried up ages ago, if I remember correctly. You have to understand," Aunt Sissy said, "the actual town of Cedar Springs was only about a fifth of what it is today, so a lot of the farmland surrounding Cedar Springs back then would actually be part of the town today."

"Right," I said. "That makes sense."

"So now what?" she asked.

"I want to see if his son Sven bought any land, as well. Let's see, he would have been about twenty years old in 1865." He did not purchase any land during that year, the year after, or the year after. But in 1869 Sven Bloomquist bought a hundred and fifty acres on the upper mouth of Poplar Creek. "It looks like Sven bought land that backed up to his father's or at least close to it," I said.

"So Emelie might be buried there?"

I shrugged. "Well, if it's a McDonald's parking lot now, we sure as heck won't be able to find any marker. But at least we know they would have most likely attended church in Cedar Springs. Maybe she's buried in the Lutheran cemetery there."

"Okay," Aunt Sissy said. She looked confused for a moment. "So, why is Karl buried in Olin, if he moved out here to Cedar Springs?"

"Probably because his wife was buried in Olin," I said.

"Oh, that's right," she said.

"I want to see the census for 1870. Now that I know for sure Sven owned his own farm at the time, he should be in it."

"Where's the census?"

"Well, I can either check the one at the historical society or I can check the one at the library, and since we're headed to the library for newspaper articles, I may as well check there."

"All right," she said. "I'll buy you lunch first."

"Okay," I said. "First I want to check the marriages. I want to see if Karl remarried and who Sven married."

I put away the land record book and got out the marriage record book. It was a huge brown volume, with yellowed pages and handwriting from another century in ink that had faded to sepia. "Oh, as usual, this is indexed by year and the groom's name."

"Good, that's what we need, right?" she asked.

"Yes, but it always irks me how the women were considered as property. You know? Oh, why would we need to record a marriage under the bride's name, for crying out loud? It's not like she's the important person in the marriage. You know? Just makes me angry."

I checked and there was no marriage record for Karl, so I

assumed he never remarried. I looked all the way up to the year of his death and there was no marriage record for him. Sven, however, married in the summer of 1869, to a Marguerite Olson. He was twenty-four and she was nineteen. "Karl never married. Sven married in 1869."

"All right," she said. "Let's eat lunch."

"Wait, I want to check one more thing." I got the land records back out and checked for the year that Karl had died. Sure enough, Sven had received his father's land. I assumed there was a last will and testament for Karl that would probably be more specific. But since he never remarried and Sven was his only child, I really didn't see the need to look it up. "So, Sven inherited his father's land, which joined with his, and he ended up with a little over two hundred acres of pretty prime property," I said.

"Well, that's good," Aunt Sissy said. "Now let's eat."

"Yeah, I'm pretty hungry," I said. "And if I don't eat before I go to the library, I'll have a severe headache."

Eighteen

The Cedar Springs Library was fairly new, with sapling lining the sidewalk in front. Aunt Sissy and I had managed to eat lunch without once talking about the precarious predicament of my stepfather. We had scarfed down our pizza, guzzled soda, made a few passing comments about poor Anna Bloomquist's life before heading to the library as quickly as we could. As Aunt Sissy pulled the truck into a parking space near the front entrance, she turned to me and said, "So, what's going to happen to Colin, do you think?"

"I have no idea. All I know is there isn't much more I can do for him. Except check out Kimberly Canton, and I don't really know anything about her or where to begin. Besides, she may have nothing to do with it all. You know her?"

"Snooty bitch from Duluth," she said, and turned off the engine. "Showed up here about three years ago, claiming to have some sort of right to the lake property or something like that. Then when nobody would believe her, she started letting money do the talking, and that worked a little better. She probably owns half of the land around the lake by now."

"Huh," I said. "Do you know who the original owners of the lakefront property were?"

"No, I wouldn't have a clue," she said. "Why?"

"Well, maybe this is a family thing. Maybe she does have some claim to some of the land through her grandparents or something," I said.

"Maybe. Whatever it was, it was thrown out of court. That's why she had to start buying it up."

We said nothing as we walked along the sidewalk and up the steps to the library. As we went inside Aunt Sissy turned to me, a tired expression in her eyes. "Far as I'm concerned, she can just take her long manicured fingernails and her fake boobs and go back to Duluth."

"Fake boobs?" I asked and laughed. "How would you know if they're fake?"

"They don't jiggle and they point due north when she has to be at least thirty-five. They're fake."

"Oh," I said and laughed. "I hadn't realized you paid so much attention to that sort of thing."

"Just gets my gall how people try to pass off being something they're not. When you get to the pearly gates, you think God isn't going to know what's real on you or not? Huh? You think you get to take those fake boobs into heaven? Hell no, you show up the way God made you. Tell you, I'd hate to face the Almighty and tell Him that I wasn't happy with what he saw fit to give me so I had to change it. No, sir, not me. Don't want to go pissing off any deities, thank you very much."

And that is why I love my Aunt Sissy.

The library was like most newer libraries. Neutral colors,

not much natural light, and filled with that wonderful smell of books. Not just the smell of books, but the smell of hundreds and hundreds of books. I wish I could bottle it. I found a librarian, told her what I needed, and she set me up with a microfilm reader and a huge filing cabinet filled with reels of microfilm and cards of microfiche.

I checked the 1870 census and found Karl Bloomquist living on his land near the creek. He had an older native American living with him, who was listed as a laborer, and Karl was listed as a farmer. A few entries later was Sven and his wife of one year. Sven owned a mill on Poplar Creek, which might explain why he was in the biographical sketches book. He was a fairly important person in the community if he owned a mill. Farmers from miles around would bring their grain and such to him to have ground into flour or whatever, depending on the type of mill he owned.

I copied down the information and then decided to check the 1880 census to see what his children's names were so that I could make sure that Mayor John Bloomquist was indeed the son of Sven. I loaded the 1880 census and found Sven and his two children.

I blinked my eyes and took another look. He had a daughter named Emelie. "Look, Aunt Sissy. He had a daughter and named her after his niece, Emelie." I looked back at the screen.

"And he had a son, John, who is most likely one and the same Mayor John Bloomquist," I said. I wrote down his age in 1880 so I could check it against the age of John in the biographies. Then I noticed that he was listed first, even though he was the younger of the two children. Then I noticed just how old Emelie was.

She was twenty years old.

"What is it?" Aunt Sissy asked. "All the color just drained from your face."

"That's not his daughter. That's his niece," I said.

"What?"

"We couldn't find a tombstone for Emelie, because she didn't die at two months of age like we thought," I said. "Evidently she lived, and her Uncle Sven took her and raised her."

"But . . . why would he report her dead at the church?"

"I don't know," I said.

"But that makes no sense."

"Well, evidently he reported her dead so that people would think she was dead. Then he moved out of Olin to Cedar Springs and raised her as his own. The only reason I can think of would be to protect her."

"From what? Konrad Nagel was dead by that point."

"I know. It makes no sense."

"Was she in the 1860 census with Karl and Sven when they lived with the . . . what were their names?"

"The Hagglunds," I said.

"Yeah, was she listed with them?"

"No."

"Then where was she in the 1860 census? She would have been about a year old."

"I don't know," I said.

"What do you mean, you don't know?"

"Not only that, where was she in 1870? She would have been ten, and yet she was not listed with Sven, nor was she listed with her grandfather, Karl Bloomquist."

"What do you mean, you don't know?" she asked again.

"I mean it, Aunt Sissy. For once in my life, I am really stumped. I guess Sven and Karl could have sent her to live with somebody during that time. While they were purchasing land and trying to set up their own farms. You know, I had a great-grandmother who lived for ten years with a family that wasn't even related to her. But both of her parents were dead. She had older siblings, but her parents and grandparents were dead, so she went to live with another family. Maybe Karl felt like he and Sven couldn't take care of her and so they sent her off."

"And then when Sven got married, he had somebody who could help him take care of a little girl and brought her back to live with him?"

"Okay, I buy all that, but why on earth would he report her dead in the first place?"

Aunt Sissy scratched her head and I stared at the name Emelie Bloomquist on the screen in front of me until my eyes watered and the ancient script blurred.

"It makes no sense," I said.

"You think they were trying to protect Emelie from some-body?" Aunt Sissy asked.

"Like who?"

"Like whoever killed her father and her grandfather," she said.

My head spun.

"Maybe that fire was no accident, either. Maybe whoever killed Konrad Nagel and his son, Isaac, was trying to kill Eme-lie, too."

"Are you saying they set the fire for Emelie, and killed Anna and Brigitta in the process?" I asked.

She nodded her head.

"I don't know," I said. "Then why hang Isaac in the barn?"

"A sick mind trying to warn them?"

"But why?"

"For the fun of it," Aunt Sissy said with a lilt to her voice. Like I was the stupidest person west of the Mississippi.

"I don't know," I said and shook my head. "I'm not convinced the fire and the murders are connected."

"Think about it. Whoever killed Konrad and Isaac may not have even realized that Anna was pregnant. Then when they found out, they burned down the Bloomquist house with everybody in it."

"Oh, jeez," I said.

"It would explain why Anna thought she was in danger. She knew she was going to suffer the same fate as the wolves. Maybe that's because she knew she was in danger and just didn't write about it in her diary."

"I don't know," I said. But in my mind I was thinking about how Anna seemed to know she was in danger. Could it be possible? I shrugged my shoulders and rewound the census microfilm. "We'll probably never know."

"No," Aunt Sissy said. "I can't accept that."

"Then *you* play Sherlock Holmes, because I'm about at the end of my rope."

Aunt Sissy stared at me with shrewd, disbelieving eyes.

"I have to leave in a few days," I said. "You have to accept the fact that I may not solve this."

"Well, whatever you can live with," she said and looked the other way.

"Oh, Aunt Sissy," I said. "I don't know these people, I'm not related to these people. All I'm saying is, if I can't figure this out, you have to understand."

"Fine," she said.

"I do have to leave in a few days."

"Fine," she said.

I made some disgruntled sound and put the microfilm roll back on the cart. Then I found the roll that had the early newspapers on it. *The Frontier Chronicle* featured an article on the murder of Konrad Nagel. I read in silence, while Aunt Sissy sulked beside me.

"How do you know she was his niece and not Sven's daughter?" Aunt Sissy said.

"Well, for one thing, she's listed as his niece in the census, which also makes sense as to why she was listed after John, even though he was younger. But she would have been born ten years before Sven got married and Marguerite would have only been nine years old when she was born. So she can't be their daughter. She has to be his niece."

She made some clucking noise and I began to read the article on the murder of Parson Nagel.

Tragedy struck the small frontier town of Olin last week. A pastor at the Lutheran church allowed a stranger entrance to his home, where the stranger partook of dinner, dessert of minced meat pie, and there was evidence that he took a bath as well, though some people think that it could have been the parson who had been interrupted during his bath. The stranger then beat his host to death with an iron poker from the fire.

Pastor Nagel founded Olin, Minnesota, in 1854, with the construction of the Olin Lutheran Church. Konrad Nagel owned over a thousand acres of land there, from which he donated over three hundred acres for the town square, the church, and the cemetery.

His daughter, Isabelle Lansdowne, distraught at the news of her father's demise, collapsed on the floor and did not wake for two days. When she awoke, she found that her only brother had been brutally murdered in a similar fashion. It is thought that the two murders are connected, but townsfolk are being questioned nonetheless.

At this time the only clues to the murder of Konrad Nagel are the missing poker, which left a fleur-de-lis pattern on the pastor's body, and witnesses who said the murderer ran from the house cloaked in a blanket and crying. For the murder of Konrad's son Isaac, there are no clues, save for the same strange markings on his skin. Isaac's body was found hanging in the barn of a local farmer, Karl Bloomquist. Nobody knows at this time why the body was hung in the barn of Mr. Bloomquist. The Bloomquist family has been questioned and all are severely upset by these events and have no knowledge why somebody would have hung the young Isaac Nagel in their barn.

I had an idea why Isaac had been hung in the Bloomquist barn. But it all depended on the motive for killing Isaac in the first place. Maybe whoever had killed him happened to kill him as he was going to meet Anna, and so it was just a convenient spot to hang his body. But why the display? And that was exactly what it was, a display. Or they had killed him at his home and brought him out to the Bloomquist barn to hang him, once again as a display or a warning. And if the article was right and both bodies had the same markings, then the two of them were most likely killed by the same person. I was all for Isaac having killed his father in a rage because Konrad wouldn't give his blessings to Isaac and Anna, or because Konrad refused to let him see Anna. But then . . . who would have killed Isaac? This way, with both of them having the same markings, they had to have been killed by the same person.

Who would have wanted both of them dead and then would have wanted to brag about it to the Bloomquists by hanging Isaac's body in the barn?

And then, if the fire indeed had been started to kill little Emelie . . . the only person I could think of who would benefit from all of them being dead would have been Isabelle Lansdowne, Isaac's one and only sibling.

"What?" Aunt Sissy said.

"I don't know if I can ever prove it, but I think Isabelle Lansdowne killed her father and brother so that she could inherit whatever it was that Konrad had," I said.

"But why hang Isaac in the Bloomquist barn?"

I shrugged. "Unless it was just to thumb her nose at Anna. Maybe she looked at Anna as one of those girls who just wanted the family fortune. You know, trying to marry way above her social status so she could become wealthy when the parson kicked the bucket," I said.

"Yes, but could Isabelle Lansdowne have hung her brother up in a barn? Would she have been strong enough to do that?"

"I don't know," I said. "Maybe her husband helped her. But she is the only one that we know of who had any reason whatsoever to kill all of them."

"And then when she learned that Anna Bloomquist was pregnant . . ." Aunt Sissy said.

"She was afraid that Emelie would be able to take her to court to get her share of Konrad's property," I said. "Either when she got older, or Anna could have done it for Emelie."

"Yes, but they didn't have DNA testing and stuff back then," Aunt Sissy said. "Could Emelie have had a shot at getting any of it?"

"Mmmm, I don't know. Maybe if enough people knew that Isaac was her father. Basically the whole Bloomquist family. Who knows if Anna told anybody else," I said. "She could have."

"But still, it's hearsay," Aunt Sissy argued.

"I agree," I said. "But who knows, maybe before Isaac was killed he left some written declaration of paternity. Maybe he confided in his sister."

"Desperate people do desperate things."

"As I have learned," I agreed.

"See? And you said you couldn't figure it out," she said.

"Well, I sure as heck didn't prove anything. It's just a theory," I said.

"So what's next?" she asked.

"I want to see Konrad Nagel's will. I should have done that before," I said. "I want to see just what he was worth."

"So, back to the courthouse?"

I glanced at the schoolroom industrial-sized clock. It said three-fifteen. "Yes, we still have time," I said. "And I need to check on Colin and see what's going on."

I rewound the microfilm and asked the librarian if she could make copies of anything pertaining to the double homicide of Konrad and Isaac Nagel. She said she would check into it for me and inform me of the costs for the search and copies. I gave her my cell-phone number and told her to call me if she came up with anything.

While I had the phone out, I called the sheriff's office. "Yes,

I'm calling about my stepfather, Colin Brooke, who is being held there. Has anything changed? Are you going to charge him or what?"

"Please hold" was all the voice said on the other line. By the time a voice came back on, Aunt Sissy and I were at her truck.

This time it was Sheriff Aberg. "Mrs. O'Shea?"

"Yes, Sheriff. What's the status with my stepfather?"

"I'm releasing him into the custody of Joe Morgan," he said.

"My uncle?" I asked and looked at Aunt Sissy. She raised her eyebrows.

"Yes. He is not to leave the county."

"But . . . we have to go home. We have jobs to do."

"He is not to leave the county until further notice. You and your husband can go home, do your jobs, if you have to. He can fly home later," he said.

"But—"

"Would you rather have him stay here in a cell? Would you rather I press charges?"

"No."

"Well, then, be happy with what I've offered."

"Did you question the person who called 911?"

"Yes," he said. "That's the whole reason I'm letting him go today. But I still want to keep him close. Forensics will have a lot to tell me."

"Like what?"

"Like the angle of the entry wound. Your stepfather is very tall. Forensics will be able to tell me if somebody that tall could have made that wound, that sort of thing. Just hold on to your underwear, Mrs. O'Shea."

"All right," I said. I sighed and allowed myself to be relieved. This was looking good for Colin. Thank goodness.

"Joe's coming to get him in an hour."

"Great," I said. "Thank you very much."

I hung up the phone and gave the thumbs-up sign to my aunt. "Uncle Joe's going to get Colin as we speak." I explained to her what Sheriff Aberg had said.

We sped through town, fueled by the glorious sunshine and the good news that I'd just been given about Colin. "Last stop, the courthouse, and then we can go home and relax."

Nineteen

The woman at the courthouse gave us the funniest look. As if she'd experienced déjà vu. We couldn't possibly be the same desperate-looking females who were just at the courthouse four hours ago. Why would two women come to the courthouse twice on such a glorious day? No, she had to be imagining it. Either that or she was taken aback by my shiner that now was turning sort of Picasso blue.

I smiled at her and went on back to the room where the last wills and testaments were filed. Konrad Nagel had died in January 1859, and sure enough his will had been probated in that same year. And can I just say that even though wills are a wonderful way to find out information about our forefathers, sometimes the language is so flowery and things are misspelled so badly that it can take a week to figure it all out. And sometimes wills are just plain disappointing. Quite often everything goes to the oldest son, who is to take care of his mother until her death, the end. Those kind really tick me off. I can't figure out why they bothered having ten kids if only the first one counted.

But wills can be a great way to find out information, especially if the deceased mentioned all of his children and even listed all of his goods. I found out just how important cows and heifers were while researching my family tree. The first things listed after the land were often *I give and bequeath my heifer, Betsy, to my oldest daughter.* I'm not lying when I say that I've seen wills that list the name of the cow or the horse, but not the daughter.

Sometimes, especially in the American colonies way back in the seventeenth and eighteenth centuries, a will could be the only way to connect a female to her parents. There were no census records back then, and quite often marriage records at the courthouse did not mention the parents' names if the girl was of age. So a will was sometimes the only way to connect a female ancestor to her parents.

And far too often, there were no wills at all, and that was just a shame.

In the case of Konrad Nagel, his will was an interesting document. It seemed that Isaac Nagel, his only son, was to take over the parish of Olin Lutheran Church once his father passed on. And he was to get most of the land. However, two hundred acres had been set aside for Isabelle Lansdowne, along with three books, the family Bible, his sorrel mare, her mother's spinning wheel, and two bed quilts. He even set aside two dollars each for his three grandchildren—whom he did not name—by Isabelle. Isaac, however, got the house, the church, the wagon and two horses, all of the household possessions, except those already set aside for Isabelle, sixty-three dollars in cash, two oil portraits of Konrad's parents, and five hundred and fifty-two acres of land, including all the land that surrounded Olin Lake. In the event that Isaac should precede his father in death, everything was to go to Isabelle Nagel Lansdowne. Isaac may not have preceded his father in death, but he died two days later, with no change to the will. Everything went to Isabelle Lansdowne. Everything. So she got not only the two hundred acres of land, but also Isaac's five-hundred and fifty-two acres. So she ended up with seven hundred plus acres of land.

Yes, indeed, Konrad Nagel had been well off. I wondered why he made a point of mentioning the two oil portraits of his parents when he had already said that everything in the house was to go to Isaac except the few things set aside for Isabelle. And sixty-three dollars in cash back then was quite a nice little nest egg!

But the thing that really got me was the land.

Seven hundred and fifty-two acres of land, including all of the land surrounding Olin Lake. At one time, Konrad Nagel had owned the entire lake and lakefront property. Unbelievable.

"Well?" Aunt Sissy said. "What does it say?"

"It says that Isabelle Lansdowne had seven hundred and fifty-two reasons to kill her brother," I said.

"No," she said. Her eyes grew wide.

"Well, Konrad was a conscientious father and at least gave his daughter a share of things rather than just giving everything to his only son. But she was to get little when compared to what she actually got once Isaac was out of the way."

"Amazing."

"Truly."

"Can we get a copy of this?"

"Yes, they'll copy it for us," I said. I wondered what Roberta would say if I told her that her ancestor Konrad Nagel might not have been a murderer after all, even though he was still a controlling, dominating jerk, but it was his *daughter*, also Roberta's ancestor, who was the killer instead. She'd probably black my other eye. Of course, I couldn't prove any of it. But she was the only one who had benefited from the deaths of both Konrad and Isaac. The only one.

Not even Anna would have benefited, since she was not married to Isaac. Emelie possibly could have inherited half of the Nagel estate, if a judge believed she was the daughter of Isaac and if a judge was willing to give her anything. But even so, little two-month-old Emelie could not have killed Konrad or Isaac. And although I believe Anna to have hated Konrad enough to wish him dead, she seemed far too timid in nature to have actually done it. And she would not have killed the love of her life, Isaac. Why would she, even if she was capable of it? With Konrad out of the picture, Isaac was not only free to marry her, she would have lived like a queen. She would have had wealth, security, status, and love.

It had to be Isabelle. But as I said before, I would never be able to prove it.

"Come on, let's get a copy of this and then head home," I said.

"Wait, aren't you going to stop by Mayor Tom's?" Aunt Sissy asked.

"Oh, yeah," I said. "Well, all the more reason for us to hurry. How will you make it home in time to cook dinner? And Colin is going to be starving!"

"I put chili in the Crock-Pot before we left."

"Oh, good thinking."

About a half hour later we pulled up in front of the mayor's office, with the late evening sun turning everything a golden-orange color. He was about ready to leave when we arrived. Either that or he wanted us to think he was getting ready to leave, so that we wouldn't stay too long. He cradled his hat in his left hand and his keys in his right. "Oh, Sissy, there you are. Was beginning to think you had forgotten."

"No, just a little late."

"So, I hear they've let your stepfather out of jail," Mayor Hujinak said to me.

"Yes," I said.

"Must be a relief."

"Yes, although I never thought for a moment that he was guilty," I said.

"Nah, me neither. Didn't make any sense. Hope it didn't inconvenience you any."

"Well, it may have traumatized him to the point that he may never fish again," I said.

"Oh, now that would be an inconvenience," he said and laughed. He gestured to a few chairs, hiked his pants legs up, and sat back on the corner of his desk. Aunt Sissy and I sat in the worn, but comfortable, leather chairs. I couldn't help but think it was a far cry better than the lawn chairs at the sheriff's office. "So, what can I do you for?"

My grandpa Keith always rearranged the words to that phrase, too. I smiled and scratched my head. Just what was it I had come here to discuss? I couldn't remember, suddenly. My mind was reeling so much with all of the Bloomquist information that I had found in the past two days that I could barely coordinate my thoughts. "Oh, yes . . . your parents bought the house, my aunt's house, in 1928?"

"Yes, that's right," he said and crossed his arms. A lot of people are a little unnerved if you start spouting facts about their family, especially if they don't know you from Adam. "What about it?"

"Well, my aunt has asked me to find out the history of her house and her land, and so I thought I would ask you a few questions about that, if you don't mind."

"All right," he said.

"Were you born there?"

"Yes, I was born in 1932," he said.

"What do you remember the most about the house?"

"I remember everything. It was the only house I ever knew until I joined the Navy. Then I came home and married my high school sweetheart and we moved into a house of our own over on the river. We lived there about fifteen years and then bought a house here in town," he said. "But I remember how my bedroom closet sloped at an angle. And I remember this one squeaky floorboard in the hallway that would wake my parents up, so when I got old enough to go sneaking out of the house, I had to go out my bedroom window, rather than out the front door! Me and my brother Clive used to keep a rope under our mattresses and climb down. Problem was, Mom kept a rose garden planted there and our legs would get all scratched up from the thorns."

I laughed and made a mental note to plant rosebushes under Rachel's bedroom window once I got home. Rose thorns might not have been enough to discourage Mayor Hujinak, but my daughter hated pain of any kind, and so the roses would probably do wonders for discouraging her from a middle of the night rendezvous.

"Do you ever remember hearing any stories about the people or the families that lived there before you?"

"Well, my parents bought the house from old Wendell

Reed, died back in the fifties. I remember him because he owned a big cattle farm and used to bring us a side of beef for Christmas. Every year until he died."

I smiled at Wendell Reed's generosity. That side of beef was probably a lifesaver during the Depression years.

"I don't know anything else about any of the people who lived there before us. Other than that there were some things down in the cellar that were supposed to have belonged to somebody who had lived there. I think there was an old butter churn, some books or papers, an anvil, I dunno, just a whole score of things."

"Why do you think those items were left in the cellar?"

"Well, my dad seemed to think that nobody else had realized they were down there, since the cellar had been damaged during a fire or something. Since there were so many of us, we needed every spare inch we could get. Dad thought we were the first ones to even go in the cellar since the stuff was left there," he said. "So Dad sort of gathered it all up and stuck it in a corner. I think he felt funny about it."

"Did he know about the girl who had died in the cellar?" I asked.

The mayor gave me a peculiar expression, and I wasn't sure how to read it. He was either surprised that I knew about her or he didn't know the story and was surprised to find it out from a stranger. He rubbed the stubble on his chin and regarded me cautiously. "Yes, we all heard the story that there was a girl who had died in a fire. In fact, my older brother used that story to scare the holy hell out of me on dark and stormy nights. Claimed he could hear her down there crying and begging to be let out."

"Let out? Like she had been deliberately locked in?"

"Well, that's what my brother said, anyway. Said she had been locked in, and so to this day she was still trying to get somebody to let her out." He shivered. "Still gets me sometimes."

"Did you ever hear her?"

"Oh, Mrs. O'Shea, you don't believe in ghosts, do you?"

"Well, no. I was just wondering if you ever heard anything when you were a child. You know, children hear things that adults don't," I said.

"Yes, because they're listening," he said. "Adults close their ears to things that children don't. I really wish we could keep that child's perspective as we grow older. I don't think we'd make as many mistakes."

I smiled for a moment. My aunt Sissy agreed with his statement and it was awkward for a moment.

"Well? Did you?" I ventured.

"Did I what?" he asked.

"Ever hear her?"

He took a deep breath and with what seemed like complete frustration nodded his head. "Yes, I heard her. But now that I'm older, I think it was just my sister down the hall crying because Ned Stevenson ran off with Louise Markham."

"Well, that'll do it," Aunt Sissy said.

"Funny how all you need is time for the unexplainable to become glaringly obvious," he said.

"What do you mean?" Aunt Sissy asked.

"When I was ten, I would have sworn it was the girl in the cellar crying. Now that I'm seventy, I've convinced myself it was my sister." He reflected on something for a moment and then he spoke again. "Is that what this is all about? The girl who died in the fire?"

"Sort of," I said. "She *is* the most colorful part of the history of that place. You know anything else that you can tell me?"

"Nah," he said.

"So, why did the property stand empty so long? I mean, why wasn't it sold right after your parents died? It stood empty for more than ten years," I said.

"You know," he said. "I'm not sure that's any of your business."

"Fair enough," I said, and held up my hands. I firmly believe that you have to pick your battles, and there was no point in ticking off the mayor.

"But," he said, and sighed, "it's not like you can't find that out from any number of townsfolk, so I'd rather go ahead and tell you so that at least you're getting the right story."

Aunt Sissy looked at me and raised her eyebrows.

"It's nothing more than we couldn't decide what to do with it. None of us really wanted it. By the time our parents died, we had all already married and bought houses of our own, except my brother, who became a priest. At the same time, we all felt entirely too guilty about selling it. It was our childhood home, after all. Finally, one year at Christmas we decided that we had to sell it and divide the profit between us," he said. "No conspiracy. Simple as that."

"Well, thank you, Mayor," I said.

"My pleasure," he said. "When are you planning on going home?"

"Well, I'm leaving early next week. My stepfather may have to stick around a little longer," I answered.

"Oh, probably not. Even though the sheriff may not know who killed Brian Bloomquist, I think he's fairly convinced that your stepfather didn't," he said.

"Oh, that's encouraging," I said. I looked at Aunt Sissy. "He must have found some forensics that pointed in a different direction."

"Yes," Aunt Sissy agreed. "But I'll tell you, I'm not very happy about having a brutal murder like that committed not ten miles from my house."

"Don't you worry, Sissy Morgan. It's not like we got a serial killer on the loose," Mayor Tom said. "You're perfectly safe."

As we got to his office door, the mayor said, "Oh, Sissy. You know, some time in the fifties, when Mom got her Deep-freeze, Dad just boarded up that cellar. Never went in it again. Have you been able to get down in there? It should have been pretty much as we left it. Those things might still be in there."

"When the Olsons renovated the place, they opened the cellar. They put whatever was in there up in the attic," she said.

"So . . . what was in there?" he asked.

"Like you said, an anvil, some papers, some of it nice, some of it junk."

"Isn't that something?" he said. "Well, ladies. Have a nice evening."

"We will," Aunt Sissy said.

Of course, the only thing I could think about as we left the mayor's office was the fact that we actually had to feed Colin, after he had been locked up for twenty-four hours. I didn't think that Aunt Sissy had enough food in her house for such an event. Well, that and the fact that Mayor Tom Hujinak had said that he'd heard the ghost of Anna Bloomquist. That would certainly make me look at Aunt Sissy's house in a different light.

Twenty

ey, jailbird," I said to Colin.

"Yeah," he said. "Can you refrain from the jokes? I'm pretty traumatized."

Colin and Rudy were seated on opposite ends of the table, heads down, tearing into my Aunt Sissy's homemade bread and chili as if this would be the last meal they would eat for a week. Rudy looked up long enough to wink at me and went back to eating.

"There's macaroni if anybody wants mac to go with their chili," Aunt Sissy said.

Colin looked up. "Okay," he said.

"Me, too," said Rudy. "Good thing I don't live on a farm, Torie. I am so hungry. And so sore. I think I could just go to bed right now."

"Uncle Joe worked you hard, eh?"

He gave me the look that said I had no idea just how hard he had been worked. I pulled out a chair and sat down next to Colin. "So? Did you talk to my mother?" I asked.

"Yes," he said. "She's relieved, although I think a little irritated at her husband's stupidity."

"Yeah, well, join the club. She's irritated with me for my little black cloud that follows me everywhere," I said. "Hardly my fault, but when she's upset there's no convincing her otherwise."

He said nothing.

"Any news? Have they got a suspect?"

He shook his head and shoveled in another heaping spoonful of chili. Aunt Sissy put the macaroni on to boil and in general went about making noise in the kitchen and acting busy. "How the hell am I supposed to know? And I don't care," he said.

"Excuse me for asking," I said.

"I just wanna go home," he said. "No offense, Sissy."

"None taken," she answered.

"I haven't seen that much blood in a few years," he said. "Wasn't expecting it. Ticks me off that I had to see it. Angers me that somebody is dead. Irritates the hell out of me that I had to ask . . ."

"Yes?"

"Nothing."

I smiled. "You going to thank me?"

He made some positively primeval grunting sound and took another bite of chili. I sat back and folded my arms, cocked my head, and stared at him.

"Good Lord, Colin," Rudy said. "Thank her and get it over with or you will never be able to ride home with her."

"I'm going to fly home, thank you very much."

"Colin, for crying out loud. She got you out of jail," Rudy said.

"I'd rather die a slow death," Colin said.

"I'm sure that can be arranged," I said.

Colin just kept chewing and staring at his bowl. Finally, when it was obvious that I wasn't going to move or stop staring at him until he said what I wanted to hear, he put his spoon down and looked at me. "Okay, the whole 911 thing was brilliant. There. Happy?"

"Jeez, I liked you better when you thought you were going to jail," I said. "Is that all you have to say to me? You asked me to think of a way to get you out of jail, and I did."

"Thanks," he said, and looked up at Rudy. "You tell anybody in New Kassel what just transpired here and I'll throw *your* butt in jail."

Rudy held his hands up and tried to stifle a laugh. "My lips are sealed," he said.

"Hey, don't mention it, Pops," I said. "I'd do it for anybody who groveled enough."

With that I stood up and got a bowl down out of the cabinet and waited for the macaroni to become al dente. Aunt Sissy smiled at me, but otherwise the room was quiet, with only the sounds of spoons clanking on bowls to break the silence.

The chili-mac was delicious, like everything to come out of Sissy Morgan's kitchen. Rudy did exactly as he said he was going to and went off to bed. Colin retired to the living room to watch ESPN or Fox Sports, I'm not sure which.

"So, who do you think killed Brian Bloomquist?" Aunt Sissy said.

"Lord, I wouldn't have a clue," I said. "I don't know anything about him nor do I begin to know who his enemies are. Or were. Maybe his wife was having an affair and her lover killed him. I honestly don't know."

She stretched and stifled a yawn. "Think I'm going to go take a nice hot bath," she said.

"Okay," I said. "I think I'm going to go and look over the diary again and all the papers I made copies of. Just in case I missed something."

"All right."

"Is there someplace I can read so I won't bother Rudy?"

"Yeah, you can either go to the study and read or you can always come down and share the family room with your stepfather."

I rolled my eyes. "Gee, tough decision."

I scooted my chair in to the table and took the back stairs up to my room. Rudy was so zonked, he never even flinched when I turned on the light to gather up the papers. I pulled the covers up over his shoulders and kissed him lightly on the forehead.

The study was just in the next room. I opened the window a few inches and sat down at the big cherry desk. A photograph of Aunt Sissy and Uncle Joe in an old silver frame sat on one side. Looked like an engagement picture. And then a family portrait, taken just a few years ago, sat next to that. I knew the picture was fairly recent because I remembered receiving a wallet-size in my Christmas card.

I scattered the papers out and started scanning them. I read the article on Sven Bloomquist that I had copied that day in the grocery–post office when Roberta Flagg blacked my eye. The article was all about how Sven had made himself a gentleman out of very humble beginnings, and, of course, it talked about the mill that he owned and operated. Then the article touched briefly on his wife's family. The humble beginnings that the article alluded to were indeed, if true, quite humble. It said that Sven's parents were both born in Sweden and immigrated here in the 1840s, right after they were married. They arrived with nothing but the clothes on their backs, a bag of seeds, and a few personal items. The family moved to Olin, where Sven's father sold a silver pitcher to purchase the land and build a house, only to suffer tragedy a few years later when his wife and daughter died in a fire that consumed the entire house.

The article went on to say that, after the fire, Karl was never the same and that his relationship with Sven became strained. Sven went out on his own with nothing. He was taken in by a family in Darby City, where he lived for a few years and worked as a laborer.

I skipped over the next few paragraphs because I have no interest in business ventures and such. Suffice it to say he bought a little land at a time and just kept adding on. Then he started his mill on land next to his father's property; the article claimed Sven had chosen that piece of property so that he could be near his ailing father and try to make amends. It also speculated that it was possible that Sven knew he would inherit his father's land, even though their relationship was rocky, and so he knew that eventually he would own a large portion of land on the river. Sure enough, when Karl died, he left the property to Sven.

I was a little disappointed. What had I thought? That the article was going to come out and say that Sven had eventually taken in his niece because her grandfather either didn't know she was alive or knew and refused to? Is that what I had expected? I guess it was, because my disappointment was almost palpable.

A cool breeze floated in through the window, carrying with it the smell of pine and dew and oxygen. It ruffled my papers and made me want to lie on the damp grass beneath the stars and pretend that I knew all the answers to all the questions of the universe. Of course, in my carefully planned fantasy, I would be lying on damp grass that housed no ticks.

I took a deep breath and picked up the pages that constituted Anna Bloomquist's diary. I scanned through the last quarter of the manuscript. Nothing really jumped out at me. It was obvious she was worried about her well-being. Statements like: *A chill washed through me this morning as I milked the cows. As if somebody was watching me. As if something dreadful was about to happen.*

Was she just paranoid? Was the fire an accident? And if it wasn't an accident, then she really wasn't all that paranoid, was she? But what would give it away? Was it merely a feeling, or was her subconcious actually picking up little innuendos and changes of behavior in people that she knew? Judging by the things that she had written, her mother became more withdrawn and quiet. She refused to be seen in public, which could have had something to do with the fact that her daughter had conceived and delivered a baby out of wedlock. But still, the diary read almost as if Brigitta was afraid of her own shadow. Not just ashamed.

Were they both paranoid? Or were they both feeling an evil that hadn't yet taken shape?

I couldn't tell.

I rubbed my eyes and sighed heavily.

Flipping the pages back and forth, I found the entry where her mother cried all day and fretted about the house in search of something she had misplaced but couldn't seem to remember what it was that she had misplaced, just that she had lost something. I checked the pages before and the pages after. The entry fell between the death of Konrad Nagel and the death of Isaac Nagel. Sven left for several days after Isaac was found hanging in the barn. I didn't think any of this was necessarily significant, I just wanted to be doing something. Three days before Konrad was murdered, Anna had gone to church with her father. She talked of how "the parson" kept looking right at her every time he said the word "sin."

I just held my head high and patted my stomach, for I had only done what all of God's creatures do . . . given love to the one I love.

Her father, Karl, had gone into Cedar Springs on business two days later, and Anna mentioned how she hoped he would bring back a nice new cotton cloth for making dresses. She had requested a plaid. She never said what type of cloth he brought back or that he had brought any at all.

Nothing. There were no real outbursts or anything obvious, other than her mother's odd behavior, but Brigitta had behaved oddly throughout most of the diary, so that was hardly anything.

It was not lost on me that Anna Bloomquist never mentioned Isabelle Lansdowne. Not once. Not by name, not by relationship to Isaac. Nothing.

I leaned back and closed my eyes, swaying myself back and forth in the office chair. Something floated in on the wind, through the window. Faint at first.

I stopped moving.

Then the sound lifted with the wind, growing louder and

louder, until the howl of the wolf was just outside the window, maybe three or four hundred yards away. Just on the edge of the trees. The hair raised on the back of my neck and arms. I opened my eyes and strained to see out the window. Of course, it was dark outside and light inside, so all I could see was the blackness of the screen and the reflection of light in the upper part of the window.

At first I just listened. Then I realized that if I could hear it, so could Uncle Joe and any number of armed citizens within a mile. I all but ran out of the room and down the steps. Colin stopped me at the door.

"What do you think you're doing?" he asked, a remote control in one hand and a root beer in the other.

"I'm going outside," I said. "You may be married to my mother, but you're not my father. You can't stop me from going outside."

"No," he said.

"What do you mean, no?" I asked, incensed. "Move it or lose it, buddy."

"What do you think you're going to accomplish by going out there? You think you're going to go out there and tell the nice puppy to please shut up? Huh?"

"Colin, I have to go out there."

"Why, so you can get yourself shot?" he asked. "Think about what you're doing, Torie. You're going out into the dark, knowing that the entire farming community is going to shoot that wolf when they find her."

Well, it hadn't seemed like such a stupid idea until he put it that way. I looked away, frustrated. "I can't let her die."

"What are your alternatives?"

"I don't know, but there should be one."

"The wolf won't listen to you. It's not going to stop making noise because you want it to. Its nature is to howl at the moon. Its nature is to be the hunter. If that brings it into harm's way, there's not a whole helluva lot you can do about it."

"But that's not fair," I said. "There should be something I can do. I can go out there and scare it off."

"Maybe. But you might scare it off to some place even worse. You might be scaring it right into the hands of the people who want it dead."

"Yes, but it's against the law to kill a wolf. It is a protected species."

"It's against the law to kill humans, too, but people still do it."

"Whatever" I said and stormed off.

I couldn't sleep all night, because I kept waiting to hear the sound of a rifle firing. It never happened, at least not within a close enough range that I could hear it. I tossed and turned all night, smelling the fragrance of lilacs waft in through the window on the constant, steady breeze of the night. I couldn't help but think about what Colin had said. About how it was against the law to kill humans and wolves, but people still did it. The sun rose, bright and crisp, and I was overcome with the feeling that all I wanted to do was go home.

Twenty-one

I was outside before the rest of the house was even awake. I just could not lie in bed any longer. Rudy was snoring away as I slipped out of the room. For the longest time I sat on the steps of the front porch and listened. I rarely do that. Just sit and listen. The birds were all chirping and flitting about the front yard. Somewhere in the distance I heard a hawk of some sort. I wasn't sure what kind of hawks Minnesota had, but I could tell a raptor's call when I heard it. The horses neighed and moved about in their stable, and every now and then the trees would rustle from a gust of wind. The smell of cedar would whoosh down out of the trees and wrap around the front porch, enveloping me in a coniferous hug.

Something was bothering me.

But I hadn't a clue what it was.

I could feel that little tugging at the back of my mind that pulls me in a different direction than I ever intended to go. Or that pushes at the back of my mind and makes me keep going, even though I don't have a clue as to why.

Anna Bloomquist could have sat here and done the very same thing at one time. Maybe she did it the morning of the fire. She had been seventeen. I thought about my family and my children. I thought about how I get so lost in carrying out the everyday events that sometimes I don't stop to *think* about the everyday events. Rachel had a choir concert last month, but did I really stop to listen to the songs she sang? Mary had a soccer game the day before we left for Minnesota. Did I pay attention to the game? And through the mass of chores of laundry and housecleaning and working at the historical society, did I really stop to understand the intricate workings of my two-year-old son's imagination? And did I ever give Rudy enough attention, or did we just function?

Anna Bloomquist paid attention. Now, maybe that was because she was seventeen and things always seem more intense when you're seventeen. But maybe not. Maybe that was the person she was. And at the time she wrote her diary, she really paid attention to the world around her. The color of the sun as it rose and the kaleidescope that it caused along the surface of the snow. I suddenly felt that I could learn a lot from a girl who had lived a hundred and fifty years ago and never even made it to the age of eighteen. And I was suddenly humbled by that.

In light of everything that had happened, I thought Rudy and I should head back home to Missouri and our nice, safe, boring river town of New Kassel. Okay, well, maybe it wasn't boring, but it was home. And home was comforting right now. Colin could always take a plane when Sheriff Aberg gave him permission for him to leave.

Just as I was thinking that, Aunt Sissy came out onto the

porch, dressed in sweats cut off at the knees and an oversized Minnesota Gophers shirt. "You can't leave just yet," she said.

I laughed. "How did you know I was thinking that?"

"I would be if I were you," she said. "But you can't."

"Why not?"

"I haven't gotten to show you a good time," she said.

"Oh, Aunt Sissy," I said. "I don't know."

"Just one more day," she said. "Today we'll go into town and partake of the May festival. Then you can leave tomorrow."

I smiled. How could I refuse her? If she were indeed dying of heart disease, I might never get the chance to have fun with her again. When I thought of my childhood and the time spent with my father's family, Aunt Sissy was the bright shining light of those memories. One time we had gone crawdad fishing down at the local creek. She had worn her cut-off pants, as always, and a big fishing cap. Before that day, I could not catch a crawdad. After that day, not only was I the champion crawdad catcher, but I could even catch small catfish with my bare hands. To this day when I hear the rush of creek water over rocks, I think of her.

"All right," I said and smiled at her. "We'll stay one more day."

Three hours later, Aunt Sissy, Colin, Rudy, and I were in downtown Olin preparing to watch the boat races. The sun was actually hot today, the familiar tightening of my skin indicating that I would be pink by sundown. Aunt Sissy introduced us to numerous people, all of whom were gracious enough not to ask about Colin the Convict or the woman with the black eye. We were seated comfortably on the portable bleachers, waiting for the races to begin—well, as comfortably as one can sit on a piece of metal—when Colin got a whiff of something.

"Are those funnel cakes I smell?" he asked.

"You know they are," I said. "Your nose is never wrong."

"Anybody besides me want one?"

"Yeah, I'll go with you," Rudy said. He looked at me. "You want something?"

"A bottle of water."

"Okay," he said.

"Oh, will you look at that," Aunt Sissy said. She held her hand up to her eyebrow to shield herself from the sun. Brilliant flecks of sunlight rippled across the lake. But it wasn't the lake she was looking at. She was looking at somebody in the audience.

"What? Is it Roberta? Should I hide or get on my boxing gloves?"

"No, it's Kimberly Canton," she said.

"Where?"

She pointed. "Right there in that navy dotted swiss dress and the big white hat."

"Oh," I said. "Oh."

"Oh what?"

"I've seen her before," I said.

"You have?" Aunt Sissy asked. "Where?"

"She was in the historical society office with Roberta when I went there the last time. Before she decked me," I said.

Aunt Sissy gave me a peculiar expression. I had no idea what she was thinking, but somehow I felt that we were both on the same plane of confusion. Before I had much more time to think about it, the horn sounded for the races. I leaned in to Aunt Sissy. "Who do I want to win?"

"These guys here," she said and pointed to the canoe-looking boat on the end. "Their parents belong to our church."

"Oh, okay," I said. The rowers stretched and jogged in place and then all got in their boat and picked up their oars. The gun went off and away they went. Rudy and Colin showed up just in time and I pointed out to them who we were rooting for. It was amazing how excited you could get for people you didn't even know. By the end of the race I was jumping up and down and high-fiving the people sitting behind us.

"That was fun," I said, rather out of breath.

"Yes, it was," Rudy agreed.

A few minutes went by while we waited for the next race, filled with small talk and weather talk. Then a woman appeared at the end of the bleachers and sat next to Aunt Sissy. The two of them talked a moment together and then Aunt Sissy introduced her. "This is Dicey. She works at the historical society,"

"Oh, nice to meet you," I said.

"It's turning green now," Dicey said to me.

"Huh?"

"Your eye. I heard about it. It's in the green stage," she said.

"Well, I guess that's a good thing," I said.

Dicey was about sixty, severely pear-shaped, more salt than pepper in her hair, but barely a wrinkle on her face. She smiled and waved a hand at me. "Don't worry," she said. "Roberta is weird. In fact, all of them are weird."

"All of who?"

"Her whole family is just a little on the strange side," she said. "Her dad eats fish every morning for breakfast. He's done that for, like, fifty years."

"Well, isn't that omega fatty whatever it's called in fish? It's supposed to be vital for a healthy heart, so maybe he's onto something," I said.

"Whatever," she said. "He stinks and so does his house."

"Oh," I said.

She and Aunt Sissy talked some more about local things, and then my ears perked up when I heard her say Kimberly Canton's name. "I can't believe she has the gall to show up at these races," Dicey said.

"Why's that?" I asked.

"Because she's a grade A b—"

"Other than that," Aunt Sissy said.

"She's just showing off. Over half of the lake is hers now," she said. "It's just an advertisement to all of us that she's going to own the whole damn thing soon. And the town with it."

"Why?" I asked.

"There's only a few people holding out," Dicey said. "And they are probably going to sell to her sooner or later. Hopefully they won't."

"What about Brian Bloomquist?" I asked.

"What about him?"

"What happens to his lakefront land now?" I said.

"That's the sad part," she said. "His widow will probably sell, which Brian never would, because she's going to need the money. Brian left behind four kids. They're going to need an awful lot of shoes and clothes and food for the next ten or so years. The marina may even go up on the auction block."

"Surely the authorities know this," I said to my aunt. "Surely she is a suspect in Brian's murder."

"Airtight alibi, last I heard," Dicey said. "She would have been my first choice, too, but she was in the cities in a meeting with, like, ten people."

I worked my lower lip between my teeth. "What's her deal? Is it personal or is it strictly buisness?"

"Who knows? She's a vulture."

"Hmph," I said.

"What?" Aunt Sissy asked.

"I dunno. Sheriff Aberg said that she somehow felt entitled to the land. Like it was supposed to be hers," I said.

"So?" Dicey asked.

"So," Aunt Sissy said, "I think I know where you're going with this. At one time, one person owned all of the lakefront property."

"Isabelle Lansdowne," I said. "You think Kimberly Canton might be a descendant of Isabelle Lansdowne?"

"Maybe," Aunt Sissy said.

"Yeah, but . . . Kimberly would have to know she was a descendant of her, and she would have to know that Isabelle had once owned all the lakefront property. What are the chances of that?" I asked.

"What are you guys talking about?" Dicey asked.

Aunt Sissy ignored Dicey. She shrugged and then brightened. "Hey, we don't know how the lakefront property ended up being divided," she said. "Maybe there was a deal that Kimberly feels was dishonest."

"I need to look at those land records again," I said. "But I'm not real thrilled about going over there when Roberta's on duty."

"Oh, I'm covering her lunch in half an hour," said Dicey. "Why don't you all come over then?"

"We'll be there," Aunt Sissy said.

"Good," I said. "We've got time for another race first, though. Right?"

Twenty-two

Just call me Special Agent Torie. That's what I felt like as I sat in Aunt Sissy's big rattletrap truck waiting for Roberta to leave on lunch break. Our vehicle was well hidden behind a big fir tree across the street and on the corner of the historical society. Dicey was going to flip the blinds on the windows twice if Roberta decided to dine in. That was highly unlikely, she thought, because it was so beautiful and the May Festival was in full swing.

So we sat and we waited. Anticipation swirled around in my gut and I couldn't imagine what it must be like to really have to wait for a person to leave a building so you could go and snoop around. If it weren't for the fact that Dicey had the foreknowledge that Roberta would be leaving for lunch, we could be here all day. Sort of took the excitement out of being a spy.

"If she doesn't leave pretty soon, I'm going to go over and throw her out," Aunt Sissy said.

"Maybe she's not going to go out for lunch."

"Then why hasn't Dicey signaled? She said she would signal, for crying out loud. If a person says they're going to signal, then they should signal."

"Aunt Sissy," I said and touched her lightly on the arm. Then I pointed to the historical society. Roberta had just stepped out of the front doors and taken off down the sidewalk, toward the lake. "Let's go."

We crossed the street as stealthily as we could, watching to make sure Roberta didn't turn around and see us or head back to the historical society. It would be my luck that she would have forgotten something. We made it to the door, knocked quietly, and entered.

"I never thought I would have to sneak into a historical society," I said. "What is this world coming to?"

"God, I thought she'd never leave," Dicey said. "She just kept talking and talking."

"How long is she going to be gone?" I asked.

"Probably an hour."

"Great," I said. I pretended to push up sleeves that I wasn't wearing. "Hand me over the records."

Dicey pulled a bunch of books off of the bookshelf and stacked them in front of me. I sat down in the only chair at the only desk in the room.

"Good Lord, don't let Roberta see you in her chair," Dicey said.

"I'll try not to. Is there a back door to this place?"

"No."

"Then you watch the front door and tell me the minute you see her."

"Right," Dicey said. She went to the window to keep watch. Aunt Sissy knelt beside me and tried to assist me in any way she could.

"Okay, we're looking for what happened to the land surrounding Olin Lake. I guess I need to see if Isabelle Lansdowne, or her husband, sold off parcels of land surrounding the lake."

Aunt Sissy riffled through some books and such, while I started scanning the land records. It didn't take me long to find what I was looking for, and when I did the hair stood up on my arms. Aunt Sissy must have noticed that I grew very still.

"What?" she asked.

"Right here, it's right here. The Lansdownes had to give half . . . yes, I said half, of their land to Emelie Bloomquist, by order of the court."

"What?" Aunt Sissy exclaimed. She almost lost her balance and fell over. "Well, what else does it say?"

"It doesn't say why, but I'll bet you dollars to donuts it's because Emelie or Sven, one or the other, took her to court and proved to a judge that Emelie was the grandaughter of Konrad Nagel. This was . . . 1882. Emelie wasn't married yet, because it's still her maiden name, but she was obviously an adult."

"You think this means something?"

"I think that if you were a descendant of Isabelle Lansdowne you'd be pretty ticked off to find out that half of what would have been your family legacy was appointed to an illegitimate girl who could have only proved her genealogy by hearsay. Her parents were dead, and so were her grandparents by that point. They didn't have a wonderful thing called DNA testing, and they didn't have official documents like birth certificates that could carry weight in a court," I said.

"So then how did she prove it?"

"I don't know," I said. "Sven's testimony probably played a huge part. But there had to be more than just his testimony."

"Anna's diary?" Aunt Sissy asked.

"Maybe, but . . . the diary was found in your house. By 1882 the Hendricksons were living here and the Bloomquists were in Cedar Rapids. How could Sven have used Anna's diary for Emelie's proof of paternity? What did he do, go over and get the diary long enough for court and then return it to the cellar? Seems totally unlikely," I said.

"Maybe it was something as simple as a written document from the father," Dicey said from across the room.

"What do you mean?" I asked.

"Like maybe the father made a sworn affadavit with witnesses and a family seal, claiming Emelie as his child," she said.

"Oh, my gosh, that's brilliant. I never thought of that. Clearly it would have had to have been something that obvious or no judge would have granted her half of Olin Lake," I said.

"Why didn't you find this when we went through the court records the other day?" Aunt Sissy said.

"I was looking for a court record of the killing of Konrad Nagel. Never occurred to me to look up anything on Isabelle and the land. That's the thing about court records. Unless you know the event actually occurred, it's difficult to know to look for it. If that made any sense," I said.

"So what does this mean?" Aunt Sissy said.

"I don't know. Do you think Kimberly Canton would know enough about her ancestors to know that half of her legacy had been given away?"

Aunt Sissy shook her head.

"Maybe she didn't," Dicey said. "Maybe she was just researching the lake in general and came across all of the information. She's had her heart set on that piece of property for so long that maybe she went looking for a loophole or some way to try and obtain the land without having to get everybody to sell it."

"Oh, jeez," I said. "She's definitely ambitious enough to do that. From what I hear."

"And then some," Dicey said.

"My gosh," I said. "If our suspicions are correct, that means she and Roberta are cousins."

Dicey gave me a bizarre look.

"If we're right and they are both descended from Isabelle Lansdowne, then they're cousins."

"That's right," Dicey said.

"Of course," I said, "Kimberly may not be descended from Isabelle. We could be totally wrong." I thought of the two of them in the historical society together, that day that I had come in. Something had passed between them. They definitely knew each other.

"So, how did Brian Bloomquist end up with lakefront property? He's descended from Sven. Sven wouldn't have had any claim to it."

"Well," Dicey said, "I think his grandfather bought it. See, eventually the lakefront land got split up."

"I'm assuming by one of Isabelle's children or grandchildren."

"Exactly," she said.

"And/or Emelie's," Aunt Sissy added.

"Brian's grandfather probably just purchased land like everybody else."

"Or Emelie willed part of it to her cousin John. Sven's son," I said.

"Oooh, I never thought of that," Aunt Sissy said.

I thought for a moment. Twisting my hair around my finger, I let out a long sigh.

"There's a map of the lake in one of these books," Dicey said.

"There is?"

"Yeah, there's a map of it from about 1900, and then we just did a map of it a few years back for the one-hundred-and-fortieth anniversary of the founding of Olin," she said.

"Where?" I asked, nearly jumping out of the chair.

Dicey pulled a book down off of the shelf, a thin book that looked as if it had been run off by a Xerox copier rather than published. It was about a forty-page book on the history of Olin. And the lake was the central part of its history. I hadn't thought to ask Roberta for a history of Olin. I had asked her for a history of the county and for biographical sketches. But not a history of Olin. Dumb, dumb, dumb.

The map from 1900 showed the lake and the parcels of land blocked off all around it, each one with a coordinating number that listed the name of the owner on a key below it. In 1900, a huge section, probably close to half of the land surrounding the lake, belonged to Hans and Emelie Schwartz. "That has to be Emelie Bloomquist's married name."

"Yeah, probably," Aunt Sissy agreed.

A small part next to it belonged to John Bloomquist. "Looks like she either sold a small piece to her cousin or she gave it to him. That's probably the same piece of land the marina sits on right now."

Then there were three large pieces of land. One lot was owned by Theodore Lansdowne, one by Frederick Lansdowne, and the last one by Conrad Lansdowne. I couldn't help but notice the anglicized version of Konrad to Conrad. Next to Theodore's land were two small lots that I assumed Theodore or one of his brothers sold because they needed the money. It was the begining of people outside of the Nagel descendants or relatives possessing the lakefront property.

The 1994 map was a completely different story. A great many of the people who owned lakefront property in 1994 could very well have been descendants of Konrad Nagel, but it was hard to say, since Isabelle and Emelie probably had some female descendants who married, and thus a different last name went on the land record. In fact, I didn't see the Schwartz name anywhere on the map, so I deduced that Emelie and Hans had either had only daughters or no children at all. I doubted that Emelie was childless, though, because in that case, her cousin, John Bloomquist, and descendants would most likely have had a larger chunk of the lake.

"When did Kimberly Canton start buying the lakefront property?"

"Few years back," Aunt Sissy said.

"At least. Maybe even ten years," Dicey said.

"Well, here's her property in 1994," I said and pointed to the map. "Look, there's a Lansdowne. Barely owns twenty acres," I said.

"There's Sheriff Aberg's property," Dicey said. "He bought his. He is not a descendant as far as I know."

The map did not show me which lots had been bought up by Kimberly Canton, though, because she had done most of her purchasing since this map was made. I tapped my chin and thought a minute. What was I missing?

Then it smacked me right between the eyes. I felt so stupid. So . . . so *blind*. The lots. B-12. The words that Brian Bloomquist had spoken to Colin. He had said B-12. And no, it wasn't a vitamin. It was a lot of land. I quickly traced the lots until it came to B-12. The lot right next to Brian's marina.

The lot that had been so rundown that it stuck out like a sore thumb that day I was in the boat with Rudy and Colin.

Lot B-12 of Olin Lake belonged to Roberta Flagg.

"Ladies, I think we need to get out of here," I said.

"Why?" Dicey asked.

"Quickly, do you have . . . um, in New Kassel we have a file of the townsfolk. You know, where they put their five generation charts on file. And then if anybody writes in and asks about those people, we put them in contact with somebody who has already researched that particular branch of a family or what have you. Do you have anything similar to that?"

"Yes," Dicey said. "Most genealogical societies and historical societies have something similar to that."

"I need to see Roberta's and I'm hoping like hell there is one for Kimberly Canton," I said.

"I'll have to access the computer," she said. "We put everything on the computer this past spring. I don't think Kimberly Canton has one on file, because I'm not sure she's ever filed one. I don't even know if she's from Olin. I know she was born in this county, but beyond that, I don't have a clue."

"Well, we can hope."

Dicey sat down in the chair, typed in a few words, moved the mouse around, and then tapped the desk with her fingers. "Hurry up," she said, and glanced over her shoulder at the clock. "Okay, here's Roberta's."

She pushed the print button and printed out a piece of paper. Then more paper and more paper.

"Sorry, it's printing the whole file. Not just that one chart."

"Great," I said.

At that moment the front door to the historical society opened.

In all the excitement Dicey had left her watching post, and neither Aunt Sissy nor I had even noticed. Roberta Flagg stood in the doorway with the most quizzical look on her face. She was happy to see Aunt Sissy, but when her eyes landed on me, it was a different story. A stubborn, almost hateful look shimmered in her eyes, and then she spoke.

"You've got some nerve," she said.

"We were just leaving," I said. "Right, Aunt Sissy?"

"Right."

Roberta's gaze flicked from Aunt Sissy to Dicey. We were all flushed and looked as if we had just been caught doing something we weren't supposed to be doing. Which was sort of the truth, but not entirely. Anybody was entitled to access to the records in a historical society, and don't let anybody ever tell you otherwise. Either way, only a complete numbskull couldn't have figured out that something was going on.

Roberta crossed her arms. I couldn't help but notice that she was blocking the entrance. The only entrance, which meant the only exit, as well. "What's going on?"

"Nothing," I said.

"Trying to prove your lies?" she hissed.

"Well, if I can prove them, then they wouldn't be lies, now would they?"

Aunt Sissy jabbed me. Not exactly the most brilliant thing for me to say to the woman whom we suspected of murder, I suppose.

"Get out!" she said.

"We're on our way."

"Were you helping them, Dicey?" Roberta asked.

"I . . . uh . . . I just found the books they needed. I have no idea what they were working on," she said. Dicey slipped the pieces of paper into a manila folder.

"See you later, Dicey," Aunt Sissy said.

"Yeah, oh wait. You forgot your copies," she said and ran over to hand us the folder.

"Give me that," Roberta said.

"Excuse me?" I asked.

"You can't have that!" Roberta screeched.

"Ever hear of a little thing called the Freedom of Information Act?" I asked.

I glanced over at Dicey, hoping like heck that she understood what I was trying to convey to her telepathically. *Get out quickly. Don't tell her anything. Cover our tracks.* I had no idea whether Dicey would understand what I meant, because I don't think Dicey fully understood what was going on. She had heard us talking about Emelie Bloomquist, but she had no idea about the story behind her. And what I represented to Roberta. Dicey had no clue to the significance of B-12. Not a clue.

Still, I noticed as I looked over my shoulder that her fingers moved to the computer and she escaped out of whatever screen she was in so that Roberta wouldn't know what she had printed for us on the computer. I hadn't had a chance to find out if there was a file for Kimberly Canton. I doubted it. Kimberly didn't seem like the type of person who would take the time to put her five-generation chart on file at the local historical society.

Aunt Sissy and I stepped out into the sunshine and just looked at each other. "You sure know how to show a girl a good time," I said. "If this is your idea of fun, you'd fit right into my world. You oughta move back to Missouri."

"Not on your life."

Twenty-three

Aunt Sissy and I were about to get in her truck when the sheriff's car pulled up next to us. Sheriff Aberg got out of his car, the sun making his blond hair look like spun gold. "Ladies," he said and nodded.

"Sheriff," Aunt Sissy said. "There a problem?"

"No," he said. "At least I hope not."

Aunt Sissy and I both just stood there, waiting for the bomb to drop. I just knew he was there to tell me that he was going to rearrest my stepfather. What he actually said floored me. "Roberta wants me to get a restraining order against Mrs. O'Shea," he said.

"What? She's the one who decked me!" I said rather hotly.

He held his hands up as if he really didn't want to hear it and on days like this he'd rather have a different job. "She just called my cell phone like thirty seconds ago claiming that you and your aunt here are threatening violence against her and she wants to bar you from the historical society property."

"Your cell phone?" I asked.

"I golf with her husband."

"Oh."

"Wait, you said she wants Torie kept from the historical society? Not away from her? Doesn't sound like she's too worried about violence or she would want the restraining order to be for her, not the historical society," Aunt Sissy said.

"Yeah," I said and crossed my arms. "Sounds to me like she just doesn't want me at the historical society. Afraid of what I'll find out."

"And what would that be?" Sheriff Aberg asked.

"B-12," I said. "Do you remember how my stepfather told you that the last thing Brian Bloomquist said was B-12?"

"Yeah," he said.

"Well, B-12 is a lot of land at the lake. And B-12 was owned by Roberta Flagg," I said.

"You're kidding."

"No, I'm not."

He paused for a moment and I found myself clenching my fists in anticipation. "Now don't repeat that to anybody and don't go getting all fired up about this. Could be a logical explanation," he said. "And I also want to request that you not go back to the historical society. I'm not saying that you can't get Dicey to look something up for you, but I don't want you going back there. Even though you're not doing anything wrong, you have to admit that your very presence is like a plague."

"I've been told that before," I said. "Thanks."

"Just stay at your aunt's, enjoy the May Fest. Go home. All right? Because if I catch you over there again, I will bring you in for disobeying an officer."

"Wouldn't be the first time," I said under my breath.

"What?"

"I'll stay away," I said.

"Great, now you and Sissy go on and do something fun. Go watch the races."

"Thanks, Sheriff," Aunt Sissy said.

He nodded and got back in his squad car. Aunt Sissy and I pulled out and headed back to the boat races. I flipped through the pages of the file that Dicey had printed out for us. "Dicey probably thinks we're loony," I said.

"Well, she wouldn't be too far off," Aunt Sissy said. "So what's in the file?"

"Five-generation charts. Roberta is descended from Konrad Nagel through his daughter Isabelle Nagel Lansdowne, through her son Frederick, through his daughter Grace." I stopped and flipped the page to another five-generation chart. "Through her daughter Isabelle, through her son Neville," I said taking a deep breath. "Through Neville's son Terrence, through his daughter Catherine, and finally to Roberta."

"Nothing spectacular there," Aunt Sissy said.

"No, but maybe there's something else. There are family group sheets galore in here, too."

"What are those?"

"Family group sheets are a record of a family. Like, I have a family group sheet for my family with Rudy. It lists Rudy's name, along with mine, dates and places of birth, dates and places of death, if applicable, marriage date and place, and then all of our children. Some group sheets have room for notes. Some charts even have a place for the cemetery that the person is buried in and who performed the wedding ceremony. Pretty cool. Anyway, then I have one for my mother and father and then their parents and so on. A good genealogist will try and fill out family group sheets on everybody. In other words, I have one on you and Uncle Joe and all of my dad's and mom's siblings. I have them for my grandparents' siblings and so on. The point is to try and document as many of a specific person's descendants as possible. I have one ancestor for whom I've documented and recorded over four thousand descendants."

"Holy cow," she said. "On my side?"

"No, my mom's."

"Unbelievable."

"Yeah, and from the looks of this file, Roberta was trying to do that with Konrad Nagel. Which wouldn't have been too hard. He only had two children and neither one of them had a whole lot of children, either. My ancestor that I was talking about had fourteen children. And his fourteen children all had, like, eight to fourteen children each."

"Men may have fought the battles," Aunt Sissy said. "But women carried the weight of the world."

"Yeah," I said.

She pulled up to the lake and showed her parking pass so that she wouldn't have to pay for the May Fest all over again. I got out, taking the file and the charts with me. I nearly tripped over a big rock because I was too busy reading the file. I flipped and flipped pages until I came to a page that made my heart stop.

"She knew about Emelie Bloomquist."

"What? Who?"

"Roberta knew all the answers we were looking for from the moment we walked in that building," I said. We walked some more. "She has a family group chart in here for Emelie Bloomquist Schwartz. Parents are listed as Anna Bloomquist and Isaac Nagel."

Aunt Sissy stopped and shielded her eyes from the sun. "That bitch. You're kidding?"

"No, I'm not."

"How could she have known? The only record of Emelie is a death record that states her father is unknown. Remember? In the church records?"

We walked some more. "She must have come across either a Bible record, or those court records, or something we haven't had access to. Private family papers, most likely," I said.

"So she knew everything?"

"I'm not saying she knew Anna died in a fire and the whole bit. Heck, she may not have even realized any of that. Just somewhere in her research, she came upon records indicating that Isaac had a daughter. Here, let me look. There's a place on this chart to cite your sources."

We had made it to the lake, and Aunt Sissy scanned the bleachers for Rudy and Colin. She found them, and up on the bleachers we went. When I sat down next to Rudy, he laid his hand on my leg and squeezed it. "Hey, sweetie," I said. It was just one of those exchanges that happen so casually but really mean a great deal.

I continued reading. "Here. Emelie Bloomquist's birth source is . . . Bible records of Sven Bloomquist, guardianship records—of course, I hadn't thought of that."

"What do you mean?"

"More than likely, Sven had legal guardianship of Emelie for a while and then gave over legal guardianship to whoever had her all those years, or something along those lines. Um . . . and here we go, court records. Bingo. Most likely that's the court records ordering her ancestor Isabelle Lansdowne to give over half of the land. That's most likely how Roberta found out about Emelie in the first place, and then the guardianship and family Bible records backed it up. I still don't know what kind of proof was offered to the judge for him to make the decision in the first place. Must have been something signed by Isaac himself."

"You really think so?"

"Yeah," I said. "Anyway, she's got family group charts documenting Emelie's descendants all the way to—"

"Excuse me, ladies," a voice said. "Gentleman."

I looked up, and it was Mayor Hujinak. "Oh, Mayor Tom. How are you?" Aunt Sissy said.

"Very good," he said. "Mrs. O'Shea, I wanted to tell you that since our conversation the other day, all I have done is think about the old home place."

"Oh," I said. "Really?"

"Yeah, and I can't stop thinking about the ghost," he said, and curled his fingers in the quote signs.

"Oh, sorry," I said.

"No, no, don't be sorry," he said. "It brought back a lot of other memories, too. Things I hadn't thought of in years. But, hey, Sissy, I was wondering if you'd do me a favor."

"Sure, Mayor Tom, what is it?"

"If I come out to your house, would you give me a tour? I haven't seen the place in years and I'd like to see it again. Maybe take a picture to put next to the one I have of it taken back in the forties."

"Well, sure, Tom. That'd be just fine. Come on out any time."

"Great," he said. "Well, you all enjoy the races."

"Oh, we have been," Rudy said. "This has been awesome."

"Glad you're having fun. See you later," he said. He tipped his hat and then he disappeared into the throng of spectators.

Aunt Sissy leaned into me. "Now what were you saying about charts all the way up to . . . what? Who? When? Come on, tell me."

"All the way up to Kimberly Canton."

"What do you mean?" Aunt Sissy asked. Her brow furrowed in confusion.

"Kimberly Canton is not the descendant of Isabelle Lansdowne the same as Roberta. She is the descendant of little Emelie Bloomquist."

Aunt Sissy's expression fell all the way to her knees. "You're joking."

"No."

"But then . . ."

"That sort of explains why—if she's aware of her heritage—that she thinks the lake belongs to her."

"Why?"

"What on God's green earth are you guys talking about?" Colin asked.

"Shhhh," Aunt Sissy spat out.

"Shut up!" I snapped.

"Rudy, man, you are a saint," Colin said.

"Guaranteed a place in heaven next to God Almighty, just for having been married to her," Rudy said and smiled. Then he flinched, waiting for me to hit him, but I was too distracted to bother.

I met Aunt Sissy's gaze. "Because think about it. Isaac was to inherit most of the land. Isabelle was only to get two hundred acres. Isaac was to get, like, five hundred and something. If Isaac hadn't been murdered, then Kimberly Canton's family would have inherited a whole heck of a lot more land than they did. When the judge ordered that Isabelle give Emelie half, Emelie got, like, three hundred seventy something acres, instead of five hundred fifty something."

"Oh, I get it. Do you think Kimberly knows this?"

I nodded my head.

"Why do you think that?"

"Because she was in the historical society's office that day. Neither she nor Roberta spoke the entire time I was there, and then finally she just left. I didn't think much of it then, except how beautiful she was, but now . . . it makes me think that she and Roberta have been in contact. I think Kimberly Canton knows exactly who she is and exactly what her legacy should have been."

"Wow," Aunt Sissy said. "You think her motivation couldn't be just plain old greed?"

"Oh, I don't doubt that."

"So that means she and Brian Bloomquist were cousins," she said.

I riffled through the charts and then calculated in my head Brian's descent from Sven. "Yeah, about third or fourth cousins." I thought for a moment. "Too bad I couldn't see the land records for the lake this year. You know, who owns what this year," I said.

"Why?"

"I'd be really interested to know just how much Ms. Canton owns," I said.

"Could you guys shut up?" Colin asked. "The next race is about to start."

"I know somebody who could probably tell you how much she owns," Aunt Sissy said.

"Who?"

She nodded in the direction of the lake. "Kimberly Canton."

I smiled at Aunt Sissy. A thick warmth spread through my chest. "I like the way you think, Aunt Sissy. I like the way you think."

Twenty-four

Of course, now that Aunt Sissy had actually suggested that I go up and talk to Kimberly Canton, I hadn't a clue as to how to begin the conversation. What was I supposed to do, ask how the monopolizing business was coming along? Or I know, how about, "Lovely lake, I hear you're going to own most of it soon?"

Nevertheless, I handed Aunt Sissy the charts, scooted down the bleachers past Rudy and Colin to the end, and jumped off. Then I headed down toward the lake, where Ms. Canton was standing in her sublime dotted swiss dress watching the races.

"Ms. Canton?" I said.

She turned to me, wearing sunglasses that probably cost as much as I paid for my entire summer wardrobe. "Yes," she said in a tone of voice that indicated I was about to be patronized. Like the teacher with playground duty and me with muddy pants and knots in my hair.

I cleared my throat. "Lovely day," I said. "I, uh, I have something you might like to have."

She smirked. What could I possibly have that she would be the least bit interested in? "Unless it does zero to sixty in a second or is measured in carats, honey, I'm not interested."

"Well, nice to know you can still judge some books by their covers," I said.

She pulled her sunglasses down and actually took the time to look at me. "Do I know you?" Her voice was missing that familiar Minnesota accent. The thick vowels were softened and the singsong lilt was gone. I imagined she had spent years working the accent out of her speech.

"We sort of met the other day in the historical society. With Roberta."

A flicker of something danced behind those gorgeous luminous eyes, but I wasn't sure what it was. But just the mention of Roberta's name had triggered it. She pulled a cigarette case out of nowhere and put a long, thin cigarette in her mouth. She lit it, puffed, and blew the smoke right in my face. "Mind if I smoke?"

"Why should I care if you cough up a lung?"

"You certainly are charming," she said. "Your husband give you that shiner?"

"No," I said. "Business associate."

She studied me a moment. "Well, what is it? What would I want that you have?"

"A diary."

"Don't waste my time. I came here to see the races." She turned and all but dismissed me without so much as a wave of her hand. Just the turn of her body said all that needed to be said.

"Written by Anna Bloomquist around 1858, 1859."

She said nothing.

"You seem to take a great interest in Olin, Minnesota. I thought you might like to have it. Since it belonged to your ancestor," I said. I really didn't want Kimberly to have the diary, but if it would help get to the bottom of everything, I would do it.

She flicked her ashes. "And what do you want in return for this?"

"Nothing."

"Nothing?"

"Well, okay, some information."

She raised an eyebrow toward me. "It's just a diary, Ms. . . . ?"

"O'Shea. A pretty interesting diary."

"What would you like to know?"

"Who owns most of the land on this lake other than you?" I asked. She would either answer me or tell me to hit the road. It was the moment of truth. I held my breath.

She smiled at me. One of those smiles that should be accompanied by maniacal laughter. I waited for it, but it never came. "Why would you care?"

"Just answer the question. It's a matter of public record."

"If it's a matter of public record, then why don't you go and find out for yourself?" she asked.

I hate it when people ask questions that I was stupid enough to open the door for. "Don't have the time. I need to know now. Today."

She turned back to the lake. The boat with the green-and-white flag pulled into the lead, and the crowd went wild.

"Come on, it's not going to cost you anything to tell me, and you get a diary in return. An heirloom."

"My weakness," she said. She took a deep breath and told me her story without taking her eyes off the boats. "Imagine being put in a foster home when you're six years old. Imagine being raised by a stranger who drank too much and his wife who cried too much. Imagine busting your ass to get through high school and college and then one day finding out that there's this nice little gem of a lake to the north that should have been yours. Biologically, I was the only child of a compulsive gambler, who had been the only child of a man who owned two hundred and three acres of pristine land on this lake. My father lost everything he had, including me, and then his property went up on the auction block to settle his debts. I decided one day to come back to Olin and find out just who I was."

"And?"

"And I discovered this woman named Emelie Bloomquist Schwartz, my ancestor, who had been victimized much as I had been. All of her inheritance had gone to her aunt. But she fought back. She took her case to court and was given a great deal of what would have been hers in the first place. I wanted to be just like her. I wanted my father's land back. And once I got my father's land back, I wanted Emelie's land. And then I decided why not have it all? It's not like anybody here really understands what the lake means. It's not like anybody here really appreciates the lake."

"So who owns the rest?"

"You know who, or you wouldn't be asking me. Roberta Flagg owns it. She became incensed when she realized who I was and that I owned half the lake. She began buying up everything she could get her hands on."

"How can she afford that?"

She shrugged. "Hell if I know. I think her husband had some savings. They sold some acreage they had out in the county somewhere. They've taken out loans. The hell of it is, she keeps it quiet. Somehow she's managed to buy a lot of it with nobody even knowing. I own four hundred and seventy-nine acres. She owns two hundred and ten. The remaining acreage is just small lots here and there owned by individuals."

"And she's never going to sell it to you, is she?"

"Nope," she said. "She'll never sell it. Because she's on some holier-than-thou quest to somehow restore the glory of Konrad Nagel's empire. She's nuttier than a fruitcake."

And Kimberly Canton ran a close second.

"So, now that Brian Bloomquist is dead, you'll be able to outbid her for his property, right?"

She laughed. "Funny how I'm considered the she-wolf around here when Roberta has been more conniving than I've ever been. Me? I walked right in and told the whole town that I wanted to own the whole lake. I went right up to the owners, offered them cold hard cash, and that was that. Not Roberta. Most of the town isn't even aware that she owns a major part of the lake. And so far as Brian Bloomquist's land is concerned, I'll never get it."

"Why? You can outbid her any day. You're wealthy," I said.

"Ah, yes. Let this be a lesson to you, Mrs. O'Shea. Power is better than dollars, any day of the week."

"Huh?"

"Roberta has power in this town. Allegiances. Alliances. She made Brian promise her a long time ago that if he was ever going to sell his land he'd sell it to her. Now, whether or not that's in writing, I don't know," she said. She threw her cigarette down and smashed it in the ground. "But if Brian's widow decides she needs money, the land won't go on an auction block. She'll sell it straight to Roberta Flagg. I'll never get a chance at it."

"Oh," I said. "How do you know this?"

"Because I've had many conversations with Brian Bloomquist. And they always ended with Brian telling me that he was never going to sell, but if he did, it would be to Roberta Flagg. So much for my lake," she said and looked out at the water.

"You own over half of it," I said. "That's not enough?"

"It's not acreage, Mrs. O'Shea," she said. "It's my history. My legacy. It's the part of my identity that was kept from me."

"Well," I said, thinking that she was overreacting just a bit. "Thanks for being honest with me."

She made a snorting sound. The most unlady-like thing I'd seen from her so far. "So, do you really have Anna Bloomquist's diary?"

"Yes," I said. "You really want it?"

She nodded. "I would love to have it."

"It's not weighed in carats," I said.

Ignoring my remark, she flipped a card out from between her fingers. "You can mail it there. Send it registered or certified. And insure it. I'll reimburse you."

"No, that's all right. No need to reimburse me. I'll mail it first thing tomorrow."

The boat with the green-and-white flag won the race, and Kimberly Canton mumbled "Damn" under her breath.

Twenty-five

We all sat outside on Aunt Sissy's porch, watching Uncle
Joe barbecue about thirty feet from the railing. The
sun was beginning to set over the tops of the trees, but it would
be daylight for another two hours at least.

Since returning home from the May Fest, Colin and Rudy
had been particularly chatty, talking about the races, the gorgeous lake, the wonderful fishing, and how, except for finding
a dead body and Colin being put in jail for a day and a half,
the trip had been really nice. Uncle Joe was particularly quiet,
especially toward me. I was assuming that was over the wolf. I
noticed Aunt Sissy kept cutting her eyes around and looking
at him when she thought nobody was watching. Great, I hoped
I hadn't caused a marital problem between them because of the
wolf. But I couldn't help the way I felt about it.

I swatted at a mosquito and cursed under my breath.

"That's Minnesota's state bird," Aunt Sissy said.

"What? Where?"

"The mosquito."

"Well, Missouri's almost as bad," Rudy added.

Colin got up and went to stand by the barbecue pit with Uncle Joe. They started talking about the horses or something. Rudy stretched and yawned. Aunt Sissy stared off into the woods, lost in thought. I couldn't help but wonder if what she had said was true. That she really was dying of heart disease. I couldn't think about it without a big knot forming in my throat. I took a deep breath.

"So what did the sheriff say when you called him with the information about the lake?" I asked.

"He was pretty surprised when I told him that Roberta owned so much of the property," Aunt Sissy said.

"Did he think she had motive enough for killing Brian Bloomquist?" I asked.

"Not sure, but I think the fact that the last thing he said was B-12 and her lot was B-12, combined with what Kimberly Canton told him, made him decide to formally investigate her. So, yeah, I think he's considering it a great possibility. The funny thing is the marina."

"What about it?" I asked.

"Well, if Roberta did kill Brian, she won't be able to buy his property. And now that the sheriff knows about all the land she owns and the whole B-12 thing, she can't really buy the property."

"Why not?" I asked her and took a sip of my lemonade.

"How would that look? I mean, if you were a suspect in his murder, would you go ahead and buy his land? That would look pretty bad, I think. Like, you murdered him so you could buy his land," Aunt Sissy said.

"Which is what we all suspect anyway," I said.

"Exactly."

I shook my head. "Man. Little friendly competition to see who could own the most land didn't end too well."

"No, not at all. Because Brian's dead, if Roberta killed him she'll go to jail. If she didn't, she can't buy the land, and that means that Kimberly Canton will. And our town comes that much closer to being Ms. Canton's resort town. I don't see that anybody wins."

"Nah, me, neither."

We were quiet a minute. Rudy got up and walked out to the field to see the llamas. They were such unusual creatures. Sort of gangly and yet graceful at the same time. They reminded me of ostriches with four legs, and they had the longest lashes I've ever seen on a creature. I took a deep breath. "I'm sorry, Aunt Sissy."

"For what?"

"I'm sorry if there's trouble between you and Uncle Joe over the whole wolf thing. I'm sorry that you're . . . sick. And I'm sorry that I didn't solve your mystery."

Her eyes glistened a little. But Aunt Sissy in all her gruffness bulled right through it, not allowing a moment for emotion. "Not your fault I'm sick. And you did solve the mystery. You found out who wrote the diary, and you found out how it ended. So far as Joe is concerned, well . . . yeah, that's your fault, but he'll get over it."

"Yeah, as soon as I'm gone, he's going to go join the hunt. Isn't he?"

She looked straight at me. "You want me to answer that, or you want to have some hope?"

"Don't answer it," I said.

I was quiet again for a few minutes, enjoying the smell of

lilacs and barbecue, pine, and . . . horse manure. "What do you think it was like for Anna Bloomquist when the wolves were killed? I mean, what was it really like?"

"I imagine she was horrified."

"You think her father and brother helped to kill the wolves? You know, they were farmers, too."

"I don't know," she said and shrugged. "That never occurred to me. I imagine they would have."

"It would have been all the more traumatizing," I said.

"Yeah. In some ways, Anna didn't seem like she existed in the real world. It was almost as if she was living . . . a fantasy."

"Yeah, like . . . everything was more real for her than it was for others. She felt joy more. She felt terror more."

Aunt Sissy nodded.

"I wish I could have solved all of it."

"You mean, who killed Konrad and Isaac?"

"Yeah."

"I thought you said it was Isabelle Lansdowne. She had all of that motive."

"I know, but I can't prove it. Besides, there's one thing that bothers me."

"What's that?"

"I'm still worried about how Isabelle was able to hang her brother," I said. "Physically, it doesn't seem like she could have managed it."

"Maybe her husband, seeing the opportunity to get rich or richer, helped her. Who knows, maybe he's the one who actually did it. Maybe they did it together."

"Yeah, I thought about that, too."

The crunch of wheels on gravel sounded from the side of the house. Uncle Joe lifted up a hand and waved. I'm not sure why, but I was half expecting Sheriff Aberg to come walking around the building. Instead it was Mayor Tom Hujinak. Uncle Joe introduced him to my stepfather. Rudy was still out in the field somewhere looking at the llamas. Mayor Tom raised a hand at us on the porch.

"I took a picture in front," he said to Aunt Sissy.

"That's fine," she said. "You here for your tour?"

"Yup," he said.

"Well, come on in," she said.

We both got up and led the way for Mayor Tom. He followed us in the back door, through the screened-in part of the back porch where my quilt still sat in the frame. I think Aunt Sissy had to set maybe ten more stitches in it, and then hem it, and it would be finished. We came into the kitchen, and Tom Hujinak stopped in his tracks.

"Oh, wow, Sissy. This is totally different."

"I expect it would be," she said. "All new cabinets, whole new floor. The moulding is the same, though."

She led us on a tour of the house then. Started on the first floor, then went to the second floor. It was on the second floor that Mayor Tom started to see some resemblance to the house he had once lived in. He went to the bedroom at the end of the hallway. "This was my room," he said.

We followed him in, and he turned a complete circle in the middle of the room. "This is pretty much as I remember it, except I had baseball posters hanging on that wall instead of that beautiful dried flower arrangement you've got there."

We laughed at that. He went to the window, lifted it, and looked down. "No roses, but you've got plenty of lilacs."

"They surround the entire house."

"Do you get a lot of bees because of that?"

"Yeah, but they don't bother us. Guess we're all too sour for them to sting."

"Hope you don't mind," he said. He walked over to the closet and indeed it sloped at a fairly steep angle. "The roof."

"Oh," I said.

He turned in the closet. "And the brick wall."

"Brick wall?"

"Part of the original chimney," he said.

"The original chimney?"

"Yeah, when the house burned, the chimney was still standing, so they just built the house up around it. I think it goes all the way to the cellar," Aunt Sissy said. "Or it ends right above it."

"Oh," I said.

"Thanks, Sissy, for letting me see the place again," he said.

"Oh, you're quite welcome."

"You guys have really turned it into a nice place," he said. "A lot nicer than when we lived here."

"Well, you know, umpteen kids during the Depression. Didn't leave a lot of time or money for home improvement," Aunt Sissy said.

"You got that right," he said.

"So, when you heard . . . the ghost," I said, "what did you hear?"

"I told you. It was my sister in the next room crying over her boyfriend," he said and pointed through the closet to the next room.

"The ghost was in your closet?" I asked.

"There was no ghost," he said.

"I know," I said. "Just humor me."

"Okay, the ghost was in my closet."

"And this chimney ends right above the cellar," I said.

"Yeah," Aunt Sissy said.

"I want to see the cellar," I said with a sudden rush of adrenaline.

"Why?" Mayor Tom asked.

"I want to see if there's an opening or something down there that might help sound travel up this chimney and into your closet," I said.

"There is no ghost!" he said.

"I know, I know," I said. "But I just wanna see."

"Why?" he asked.

"Because I'm morbid," I said.

"All right," Aunt Sissy said. "Let's go to the cellar. You coming with?"

Mayor Tom turned a pasty white around his mouth. He swallowed. "All right," he said.

We all three descended the steps, me in the lead because I just suddenly had to see what the cellar looked like, Mayor Tom reluctantly pulling up the rear, and my aunt sandwiched in the middle. Once out on the back porch, Aunt Sissy had to move some things aside and then she pulled the door up and fixed it to a hook on the wall, designed specifically for that. Then she flipped a switch on the wall. "Took us forever to realize that switch was for the light down there."

"I'll bet," I said.

The steps were little more than a ladder. They were actually stairs that descended almost vertically. As I went down the stairs, I had to duck my head so I wouldn't knock it on the floor of the back porch.

"There is a concrete floor down here now. I don't think there would have been one when Anna lived here."

"No, probably not," Tom said from behind her.

I immediately started itching when I got down in the room. It felt like things were crawling in my hair and up my arms. Psychosomatic, but it's hard to remember that when your skin is crawling. I was just glad that I was with two other people. I figured they could save me from whatever multilegged thing might attack me.

The room was small, maybe ten feet by ten feet. With a house as big as Aunt Sissy's one would expect a larger cellar. But that's not how they did it back in the old days. A cellar was mainly used to store food or to offer protection from tornadoes and dust storms. Not that Minnesota would be bothered by too many dust storms.

The ceiling was barely six feet high, and Mayor Tom sort of held himself in a semihunched position, watching the ceiling for anything that might decide to nest in his hat. I, too, watched the ceiling with keen interest. It didn't seem to be moving. Yet.

"We turn the light on down here once in a while, just to scare the spiders," Aunt Sissy said.

I gave a nervous laugh.

"Okay, so you've seen the cellar. Let's go," Mayor Tom said.

"Wait, where's the fireplace?"

"It would be right there," he said and pointed to the ceiling at the end of the cellar.

I walked over and tried to get a good look, but the light cast severe shadows, and the corners of the room were dark. But a spark of light in the ceiling caught my eye. "Wait. One of you run up to the fireplace in the living room."

"What are you going to do?"

"I'm going to stick a pen or something up through this hole and you tell me if you can see it."

Aunt Sissy went up the steps.

"Are you there yet?" I yelled.

"Yes," she called back.

I realized that once again in my life, I was not tall enough. Mayor Tom instantly understood and came over and stuck a ballpoint pen through the hole. "You see it?" he yelled.

"No . . ." she said. "Oh, wait. Yes."

A minute later she came back down the steps. "Where the brick meets the wall, there's a small hole in the floor. You can't really see it, unless you're looking for it. That might explain where all of our eight-legged friends are coming from."

"So, what does it mean?" Mayor Tom asked.

I shrugged. "Maybe nothing," I said. "It's just that if the door to the cellar were shut, you should be able to hear whoever was in there. It would most likely travel up the brick."

"So you're saying there was a ghost," Mayor Tom said. "Sissy, no offense, but you have the most bizarre family."

She just shrugged.

"No, I'm not saying that there was a ghost."

I looked around a moment, and then I was ready to go. Mayor Tom hesitated.

"What?"

He stared at the wall for a second. "What's that?"

"What's what?" I asked.

"There's something written on the wall . . . I can't make it out. Sissy, you got a flashlight?"

"Yes," she said. "I'll be right back."

I leaned down in front of where he was pointing and tried

243

to see what it was, but I just couldn't make it out no matter how much I strained my eyes. Aunt Sissy returned with a flashlight and shined it on the wall. There, scraped into the stone were four letters.

P.

A.

Another P. And another A.

Papa.

"Oh, my God, I'm going to be sick," I said.

"What is it?"

Tears welled in my eyes and my breath came in quick, ragged gasps. "Papa. It was her father."

"What was her father?" Tom asked.

Aunt Sissy just stared at me, still not comprehending. Why I hadn't even suspected was beyond me. Anna's diary talks about how her father was gone from home the night of Konrad Nagel's murder. Describes her mother's bizarre behavior afterward. The fact that Sven had been the one to report the deaths. The fact that Karl Bloomquist had not taken his granddaughter in. He had never taken in Emelie Bloomquist because he thought she was dead. Sven had found a couple who would raise her away from Karl, and only when Karl was dead did Sven bring her to live with him. It was Karl whom they had been afraid of all along.

I had to wonder if Anna had figured it out. That her father had been the one to kill her lover and his father.

"Karl Bloomquist killed Konrad, most likely because Konrad refused to let Isaac marry Anna."

"And then he killed Isaac for getting her pregnant in the first place?" Aunt Sissy asked.

"That would be my guess."

"Who are you guys talking about?" Mayor Tom asked.

"And then he burned down the house with his daughter and her baby inside, hoping to rid himself of the whole distasteful deed," Aunt Sissy said.

"Only he didn't realize his wife was inside. Or maybe he did and by then he didn't care," I said.

"Oh, my God," Aunt Sissy said.

"Yeah," I said.

"Who are you guys talking about?" Mayor Tom insisted.

"Your ghost," I said. "And her tragic life."

"There is no ghost," Tom said.

"I've gotta get out of here. The mold and mildew is making me sick," I said.

"I'm with you," Mayor Tom said.

Within seconds we were out of the cellar and on the back porch. I shivered from the overwhelming betrayal of it all. I put my head between my knees and just cried. I cried for Anna Bloomquist, who had clawed her killer's name on the cellar wall as she succumbed to the ghastly black smoke.

"Are you guys gonna tell me what is going on?" Mayor Tom asked.

Aunt Sissy put a hand on my shoulder and I swiped at my tears. I took a deep breath and tried to calm myself. It might not ever stand up in a court of law, but I knew in my gut that Karl Bloomquist was the killer of Konrad and Isaac Nagel and his own daughter and wife.

"Aunt Sissy," I said.

"Yes?"

"Next time you want to know who wrote something? You

find it out for yourself. This has been the most gut-wrenching thing I've been through in a long time. And I don't even know these people!"

"Next time I find an ancient diary, I'm not even going to read it."

Twenty-six

I tossed and turned all night. Partly because I knew we were leaving the next day, and partly because I was sleeping in the house on the site where a zealot had burned down his house so that his daughter and grandaughter would no longer be an embarrassment to him. Oh, and then there was Brian Bloomquist, who I would bet money was murdered simply because he owned a tract of land that Roberta Flagg wanted.

Thoughts of Roberta and her audacity kept my heavy eyes wide open for hours. The woman had the audacity to punch me because I dared to say something negative about her ancestor. He wasn't a murderer, but he was certainly a jerk. I couldn't take it any longer. Maybe it was my ego, but I could not let that woman think she had pulled the wool over my eyes. Maybe she had everybody else in this town fooled, but she didn't fool me.

I got up at six, skipped breakfast, and borrowed Rudy's truck. I drove around the country, around the lake, through town, and then I eventually stopped at the side of the lake without buildings and without people and just sat there surrounded by Mother Nature and tried to clear my head. The lake was gorgeous, the blue sky reflected on the surface, with the green trees lining the side. It almost looked like I was at one of those IMAX movies where everything was projected in a circle all around me.

Finally, I went to the historical society hoping to find Roberta. She wasn't there. It was too early. I went to a gas station and looked in the white pages and found Roberta's address. Then I asked the attendant where Watson Grove was located.

When I knocked on her door a few minutes later, I was keenly aware of the little things, like the bikes that were thrown down in the yard, the sandbox. The dog doo I had just stepped in. It was a small ranch, probably three bedrooms. They couldn't afford much. How could they? Every penny they had was being spent on lakefront property. Roberta answered the door wearing a dingy plaid house robe and big pink fluffy slippers. She looked shocked to see me. There was a sense of satisfaction hidden in that expression of shock. Like she was going to get one more chance to deck me or something.

"I want to talk to you," I said.

"I'm not letting you in my house for love or money," she said.

"I need to talk to you about Brian Bloomquist," I said.

Roberta gave a nervous look over her shoulder. "I have nothing to say," she said.

Her family was probably at home. She wasn't going to talk to me where they could hear her, no matter what.

"Why don't you come out here on the porch," I said. "That way I can call you a murderer, and your kids won't hear me."

Roberta's face went white. Then she laughed. "I have no idea what you're talking about."

"I think you do," I said.

She shut the door and came out on the porch then. "Say what you have to say and then get off my property, out of Olin, and out of this state."

"In a hurry to get rid of me, eh?"

She exhaled an angry breath and then said, "What do you want?"

"I just want to let you know that you don't fool me. I know you killed Brian Bloomquist," I said. "You thought if you killed him everybody would automatically assume it was Kimberly Canton. Then you'd be free to buy the property. What you didn't think of . . . which either shows your haste or your stupidity—I'm going for the latter—is that Kimberly Canton has an airtight alibi."

She said nothing.

"So, then you're still free to buy the land—if the widow decides to sell—because nobody really suspects little ol' Roberta. You've been very quiet about the subject."

"What subject?"

"The fact that you're in a race to get as much lakefront property as Kimberly Canton."

"Don't be silly," she said, but she pulled her robe closer to her chest.

"You own over two hundred acres right now, isn't that right?" Roberta's gaze shifted from mine to somewhere in the front yard. "But you didn't figure anybody would ever catch on to that, did you?"

She said nothing. Anger seethed from every pore, but she said nothing to me.

"And nobody would have, if my aunt hadn't found that diary and started snooping around," I said. "Now everybody knows everything."

"What do you mean?" she asked.

"I mean, I've told the sheriff everything I know and all of my suspicions," I said.

She laughed then, relief washing over her. "Oh, is that all? Ooooh, I'm shivering here. Go home, Mrs. O'Shea."

I stopped her from turning to go inside by grabbing her arm, and she looked down at my hand as if it were diseased. "Get your hand off of me," she said. "You're not in your hometown, dearest. You're in Olin. My town. They can't arrest me on your suspicions. I don't know how they do things in Missouri, but in Minnesota we have to have a little thing called physical evidence."

I leaned in close to her then. "Oh, I'm not saying you're going to be brought up on charges. I'm just here to let you know that I know, Roberta. I know what you are and I know what you did. Whether I can prove it or not."

Still Roberta said nothing. A flicker of something danced through her eyes. Fear. Guilt. And then justification. She felt justified in what she had done.

"And that's what I came here for," I said.

"What?"

"That look you just gave me. My proof," I said and let go of her arm.

I turned and walked down her steps, turning back to add one last thing. "Good day, Mrs. Flagg. You better hope you didn't leave any of that 'physical evidence' behind."

With that I got in my husband's truck and headed back to

my aunt's farm. I was satisfied now. I knew by the look on her face she was guilty. Oh, and the fact that less than thirty seconds after I pulled out of her driveway she threw her kids in her car and took off like a bat out of hell. Still in her pajamas.

Twenty-seven

I went back to Aunt Sissy's, and after having one of her fabulous breakfasts of all breakfasts—reheated—Rudy and I started to pack the truck. A call came from the sheriff's office for Colin. I stood in the kitchen and watched my stepfather almost melt into a puddle of relief as he listened to Sheriff Aberg on the other end. He hung up the phone and then gave a gleeful shout.

"I get to go home with you guys. All charges dropped. I can leave the state. I can go home to my wife and . . . and . . . I get to ride in a car with you for twelve hours," he said.

I smiled.

"I didn't think I would ever be so happy to be stuck in a truck with you for twelve hours, but, by golly, I can't think of anything else I'd rather be doing," he said.

"Not even fishing?" I said.

"Okay, well, no point in going to extremes."

Aunt Sissy had been standing at the doorway. "I'm glad you

get to go home with Rudy and Torie. Did they happen to say why they were letting you go?" she asked.

"Yeah," he said. "They made another arrest."

Aunt Sissy and I looked at each other.

"Roberta Flagg."

"I knew it," Aunt Sissy said.

I sighed to myself, content. You know, it's just a lake. It's just land. It's not worth killing somebody over. How do people get so far gone in their dementia that they lose sight of that?

"Evidently, after you guys talked to him yesterday he was watching Roberta's house," he said. "And some forensics just came back from the lab."

"How do you know he was watching her house?" I asked.

"He said they arrested her as she was trying to flee town," he said. "This morning."

"That had to be hard for Sheriff Aberg," I said. "Considering he's such good friends with her husband and all."

"Yeah," Colin nodded. "It's always harder when there's a personal connection."

I just stared at him.

"Sometimes that personal connection actually makes it easier to arrest them," he said and smiled.

"Yeah, I was waiting for that," I said.

Suddenly an expression akin to that worn by a child on Christmas morning spread across his face. "Oh, I have to go pack!" And off he went.

Aunt Sissy disappeared for a second, holding up her finger. She returned with my quilt all folded neatly. "Here," she said. "I finished it for you."

"When did you find time to do that?"

"Last night after you went to bed," she said.

"Oh, I want to see it. Let's lay it out on the floor in the living room."

Once the quilt was spread out perfectly on the living room floor, without a single wrinkle, I just stood in awe. I hugged Aunt Sissy with everything I had. "Thank you so much," I whispered.

"It's personalized," she said.

"What do you mean?"

"Look," she said and held up a corner. There she had quilted in the words: *For Torie. Thanks for our adventure and for solving my mystery. Aunt Sissy.* "So that you'll never forget Anna Bloomquist," she said.

"I don't think that's possible," I said. I swiped at another blasted tear. "I will never forget her."

I folded the quilt and ran my fingers across the stitches. "You have the package ready for Kimberly Canton?"

"Yes," she said. "All I have to do is take it to the post office."

"Great."

Rudy came in then. "We're all set. We just have to wait for Colin to get his things in the truck."

I went outside on the porch to soak in my aunt's farm one last time before heading home to Missouri, keenly aware that if Aunt Sissy was dying this might be the last time I ever saw it. And her. Though I would have opportunities to see her at reunions and weddings. But I might not make another trip up here before she actually . . .

I saw Uncle Joe come around the corner. He waved to me. I took the steps down and then walked around the corner of the house. "Uncle Joe. Thanks for putting us up for the week."

"Yeah, you caused quite a stir in town."

"Sorry."

"So, you think Sissy's going to go back to normal now? You think you got to the bottom of whatever was bothering her?" he asked.

I glanced back at the house. "Yeah, I think so." The birds chirped in the distance, their music so soothing and so comforting. "Uncle Joe."

"Yes?"

"Just . . . be nice to her every now and then. For no reason," I said. What else was I supposed to say? It wasn't my place to tell him that she was dying. If she wanted him to know, she'd tell him. If I told him without her permission, she might not ever speak to me again. And she meant far too much to me to jeopardize our relationship.

"All right," he said and nodded.

I was going to reinforce how important it was not to kill the wolf, but decided not to. It wouldn't do any good. If he was going to kill her, he'd kill her. Nothing I would say would matter. People don't change their minds about things overnight or because some nosy whippersnapper from out of town made them "see the light." That just didn't happen.

Colin came out of the front door with a burst of energy, threw his suitcase in the back of the truck, and said, "Let's go."

"Bye, Uncle Joe." I gave him a firm hug.

"Ya'll drive careful."

"We will."

Colin held up a hand to Uncle Joe. "Thanks for having us."

Uncle Joe nodded.

I got in the cab of the truck and sandwiched myself in between Rudy and Colin, just like when we were driving up here. Only this time I had a full-sized quilt on my lap. And a cooler full of dead fish in the back. We waved at Aunt Sissy standing on the porch, and Rudy gave a tap on the horn just as we pulled out of her driveway.

"We taking Iowa or Wisconsin home?" Colin asked.

I rolled my eyes.

"For God's sake, take Wisconsin so he'll have plenty of places to eat."

"All right," Rudy said.

Within a split second, Colin gasped and Rudy slammed on the brakes. "Is that . . . ?"

When my head had recovered from whiplash, I looked in the bush on the side of the road. A head popped up and the golden eyes caught the sun. Then the wolf stood and looked into the woods. Then back at us and then across the road.

Nobody in the cab of the truck said a word. We all held our breath. Suddenly two little furry fat wolves crossed the road as the female wolf sort of jaunted back across the road to try and help her cubs scurry across. I knew that a wolf this close to civilization was facing an uncertain future at best. If hunters, poachers, or farmers didn't kill them, a car would. It was sort of inevitable. The problem with wild animals was once they became used to humans, then they were more likely to be killed. The passing cars no longer seemed all that dangerous, and they stopped to linger on the road.

Rudy, Colin, and I all seemed to let out a collective breath. Rudy gave the truck gas and started to go. I reached for the camera in the glove box, twisted around in the seat, and got a picture out the back window. The mother wolf just stood there for a second. As if trying to convey something to me. She seemed to be as enthralled with me as I was with her.

I kept staring out that rearview side mirror until I could no longer see her. I knew that I would never forget her. Just as I would never forget Anna Bloomquist. How could I? The two were so intertwined that I would never think of one without thinking of the other.

I turned around finally. Rudy put his hand on my knee. "She'll be all right," he said. "She's survived this long."

"Yeah, maybe she'll head back north. Or just become invisible again," Colin said.

"Maybe," I said.

"Or maybe your uncle will come around," Colin said.

I rolled my eyes.

"Look, I'm trying to help," he said.

"I know."

The annoying electronic notes of "Take Me Out to the Ball Game" played from Rudy's belt clip. He reached for his cell phone and glanced at the window. "It's your mother," he said.

"Hmm," I said and glanced at Colin as if to indicate that he was in trouble of some sort.

"Hello?" Rudy said. He came to an intersection and looked confused. Colin and I both pointed in the direction to go. The only problem was we pointed in *different* directions.

"No, it's left," I said.

"No, it's not," Colin argued. "He needs to make a right out of here."

"If he made a right he'd end up in Duluth. He needs to go left."

"No, Torie. Look, I am a man. And if there's one thing I know, it's directions."

"Look, Bozo—"

"Torie," Rudy said.

"What!"

"That was . . . your mom."

"Yes, I know, you said that already. What did she want?" A sinking sensation settled in my chest and stomach. My breath caught in my throat. "What is it?" I persisted.

"It's your boss. Sylvia," he said.

"What about her?"

"She's dead."

"That's not possible. Sylvia is immortal," I said.

Rudy looked over my head at Colin and I could tell by the seriousness of his brown eyes that he wasn't joking.

"No, Torie. She's dead. Elmer's got the morgue holding off until you can get there," he said.

"What do you mean?"

"They're waiting for you to decide on the funeral arrangements."

"Why?" I asked, tears rolling down my cheeks for the third time in two days. "Why me?"

"Because she left you everything," he said. "Her money, her possessions, the Gaheimer House. All of it."